— William Shakespeare's —
Macbeth

adapted by **Joeming Dunn**
illustrated by **David Hutchison**

magic
wagon

visit us at
www.abdopublishing.com

Published by Magic Wagon, a division of the ABDO Publishing Group, 8000 West 78th Street, Edina, Minnesota 55439. Copyright © 2009 by Abdo Consulting Group, Inc. International copyrights reserved in all countries. All rights reserved. No part of this book may be reproduced in any form without written permission from the publisher.
Graphic Planet™ is a trademark and logo of Magic Wagon.

Printed in the United States of America, North Mankato, Minnesota.
012009 062012

Adapted by Joeming Dunn
Illustrated by David Hutchison
Edited by Stephanie Hedlund and Rochelle Baltzer
Interior layout and design by Antarctic Press
Cover art by David Hutchison
Cover design by Neil Klinepier

Library of Congress Cataloging-in-Publication Data

Dunn, Joeming W.
    William Shakespeare's Macbeth / adapted by Joeming Dunn; illustrated by David Hutchison.
        p. cm. -- (Graphic Shakespeare)
    Summary: Retells, in comic book format, Shakespeare's play about a man who kills his king after hearing the prophesies of three witches.
    ISBN 978-1-60270-190-8
    1. Graphic novels. [1. Graphic novels. 2. Shakespeare, William, 1564-1616--Adaptations.] I. David Hutchison, 1974- ill. II. Shakespeare, William, 1564-1616. Macbeth. III. Title. IV. Title: Macbeth.

PZ7.7.D86Wg 2008
741.5'973--dc22

                                                                2008010741

Table of Contents

Cast of Characters

Duncan
King of Scotland

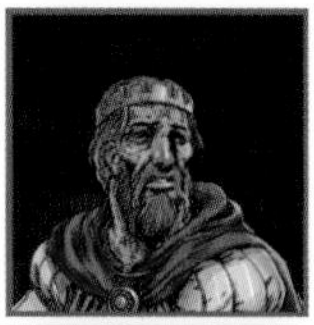

Donalbain
Son of Duncan

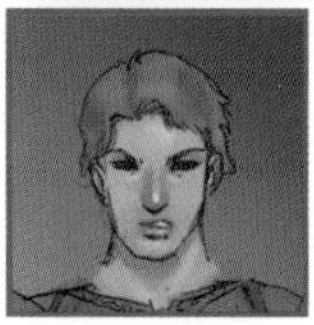

Malcolm
Son of Duncan

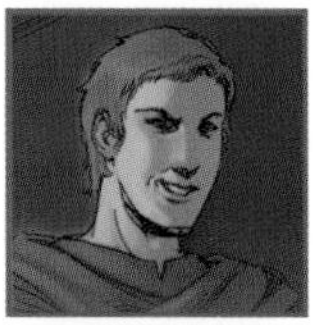

Macbeth
General of Scottish army

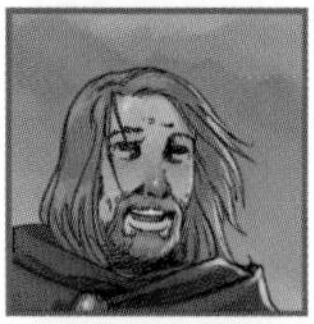

Banquo
General of Scottish army

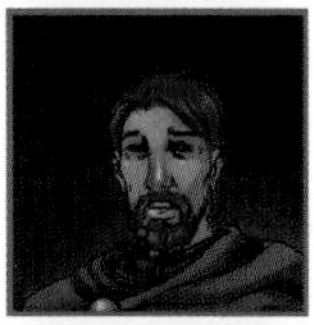

Macduff
Scottish noble

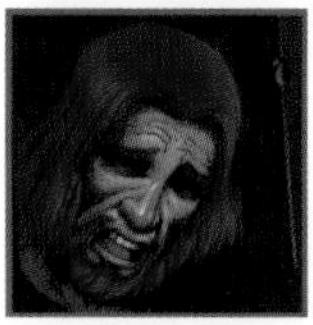

Lennox
Scottish noble

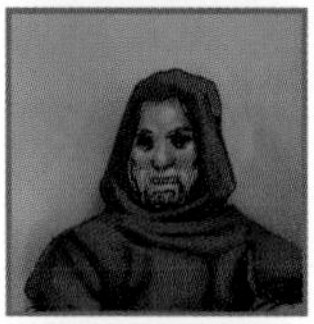

Lord Rosse
Scottish noble

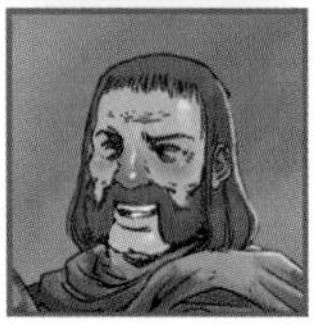

Menteth

Angus

Caithness
Scottish nobles

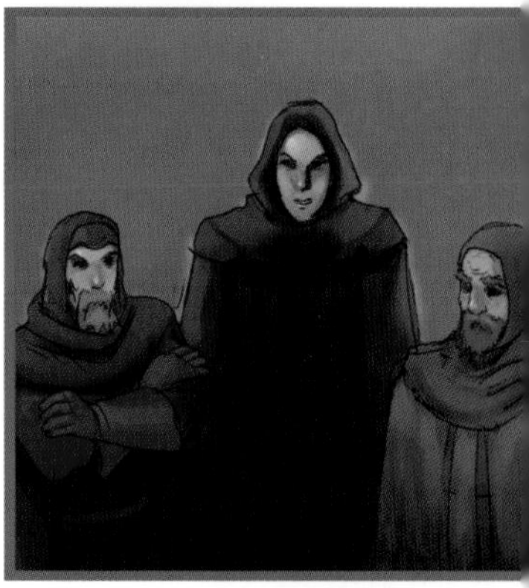

Lady Macbeth
Wife of Macbeth

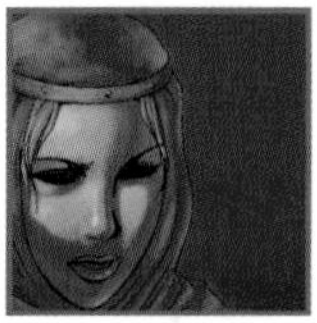

Three Assassins

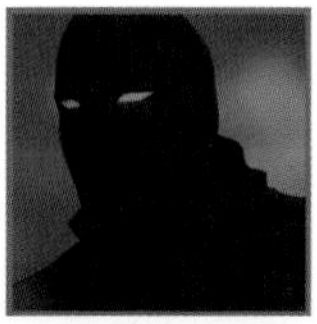

Three Witches
Foretellers of Fate

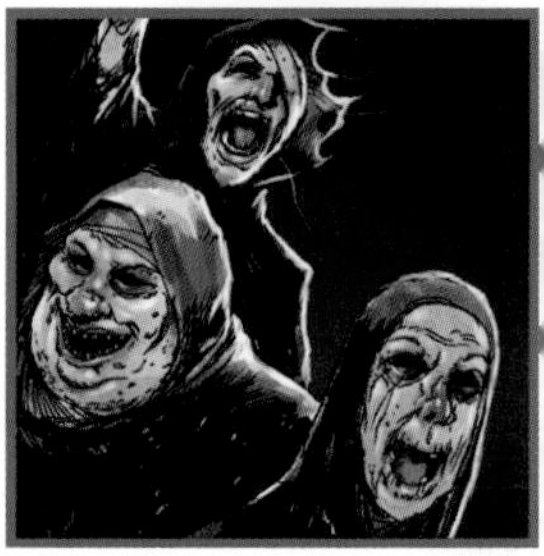

Our Setting

Macbeth is set in Scotland. Scotland is a country in the United Kingdom. It is located on the island of Great Britain.

In about 8,000 BC, the first hunters entered the land that is now Scotland. These Celtic people brought tools and weapons. In the AD 100s, Romans ruled the Scottish people. Then as England became a unified country, the English also fought to take over Scotland.

Macbeth is set in 1040, when Scotland was fighting to be an independent country. It is the adapted story of the general Macbeth and his fight for the throne. Shakespeare uses several Scottish locations for his play, including Birnam Wood and the county of Fife.

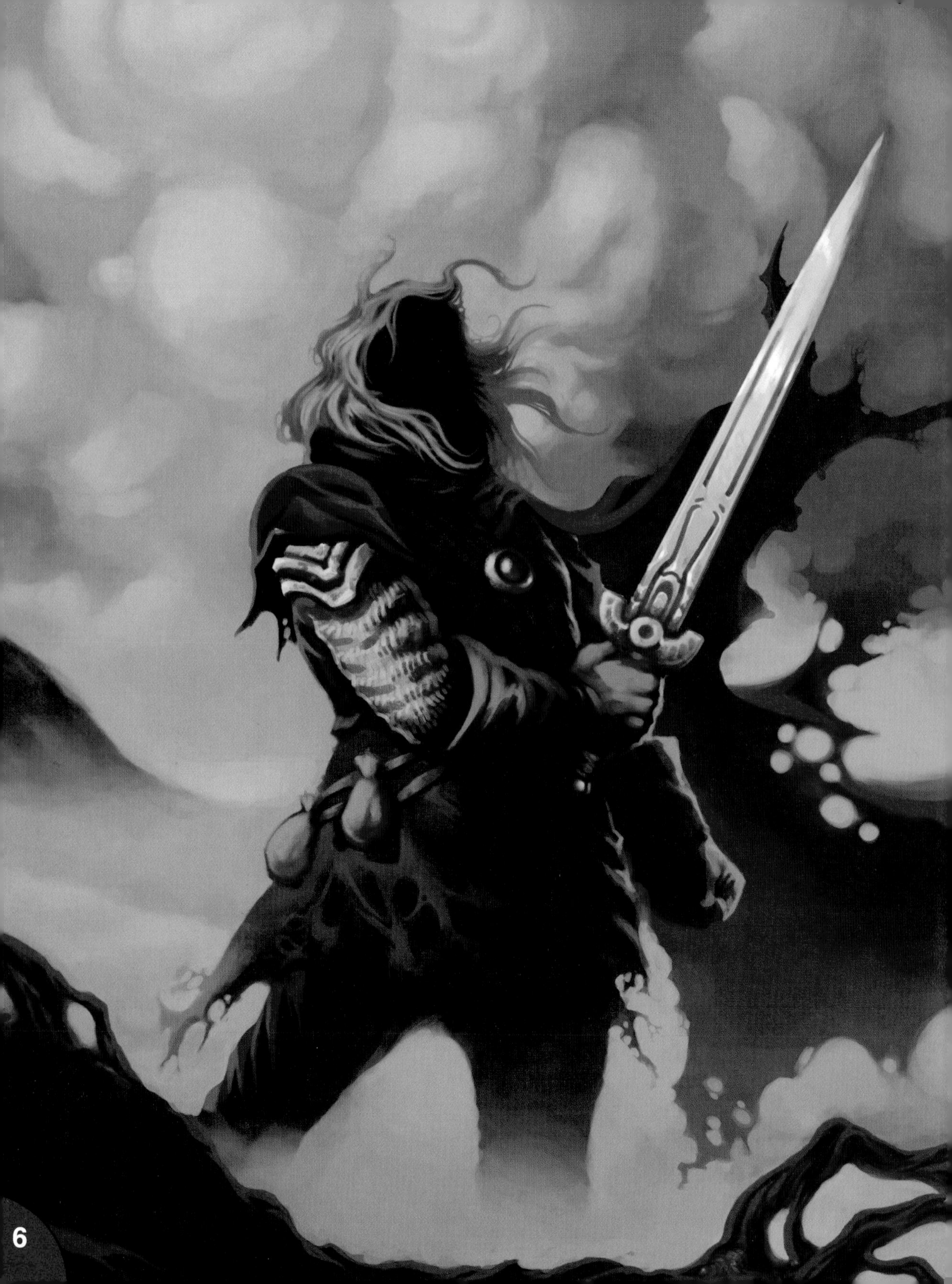

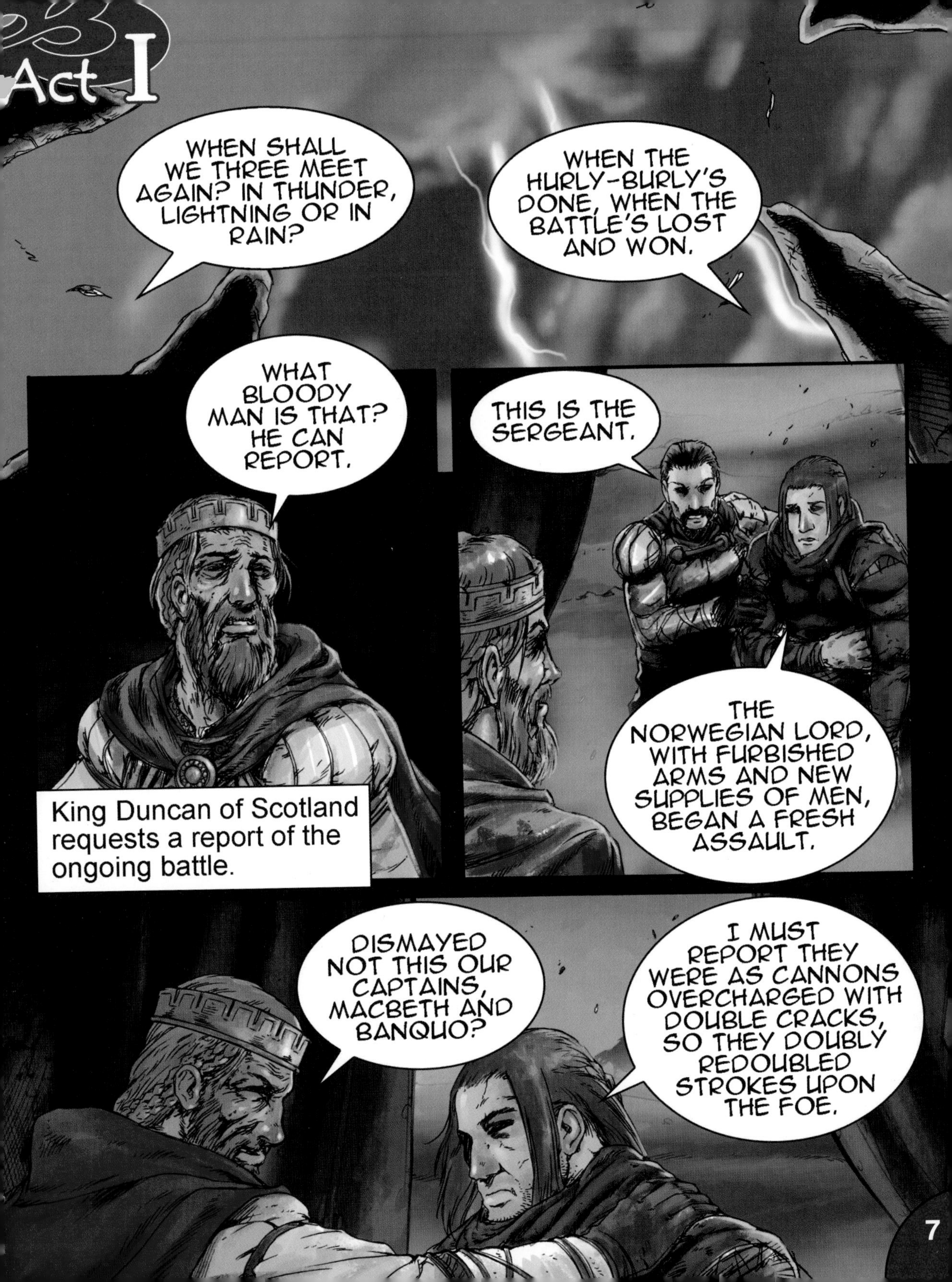
Act I
WHEN SHALL WE THREE MEET AGAIN? IN THUNDER, LIGHTNING OR IN RAIN?
WHEN THE HURLY-BURLY'S DONE, WHEN THE BATTLE'S LOST AND WON.
WHAT BLOODY MAN IS THAT? HE CAN REPORT.
King Duncan of Scotland requests a report of the ongoing battle.
THIS IS THE SERGEANT.
THE NORWEGIAN LORD, WITH FURBISHED ARMS AND NEW SUPPLIES OF MEN, BEGAN A FRESH ASSAULT.
DISMAYED NOT THIS OUR CAPTAINS, MACBETH AND BANQUO?
I MUST REPORT THEY WERE AS CANNONS OVERCHARGED WITH DOUBLE CRACKS, SO THEY DOUBLY REDOUBLED STROKES UPON THE FOE.

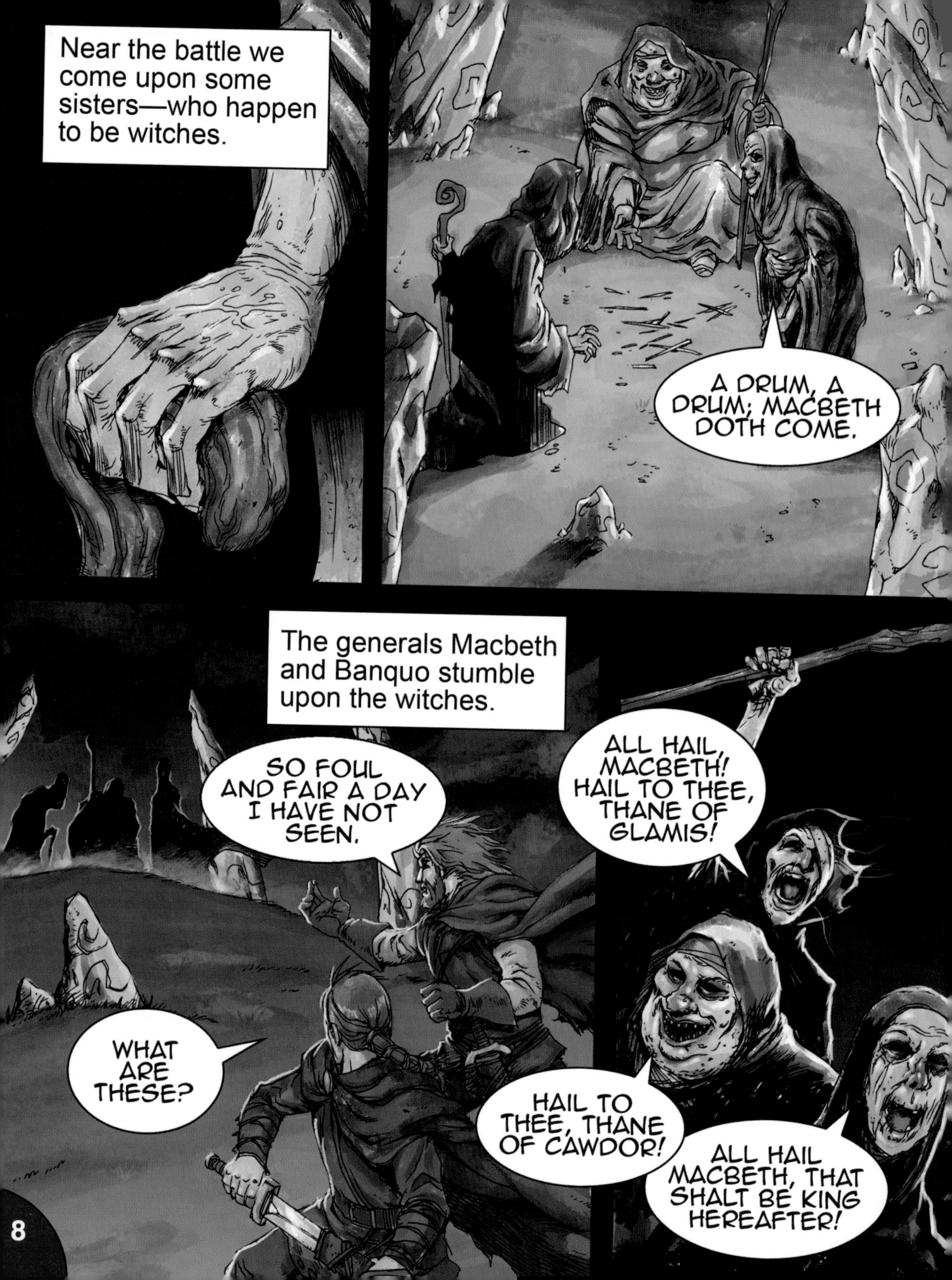
Near the battle we come upon some sisters—who happen to be witches.
A DRUM, A DRUM; MACBETH DOTH COME.
The generals Macbeth and Banquo stumble upon the witches.
SO FOUL AND FAIR A DAY I HAVE NOT SEEN.
WHAT ARE THESE?
ALL HAIL, MACBETH! HAIL TO THEE, THANE OF GLAMIS!
HAIL TO THEE, THANE OF CAWDOR!
ALL HAIL MACBETH, THAT SHALT BE KING HEREAFTER!

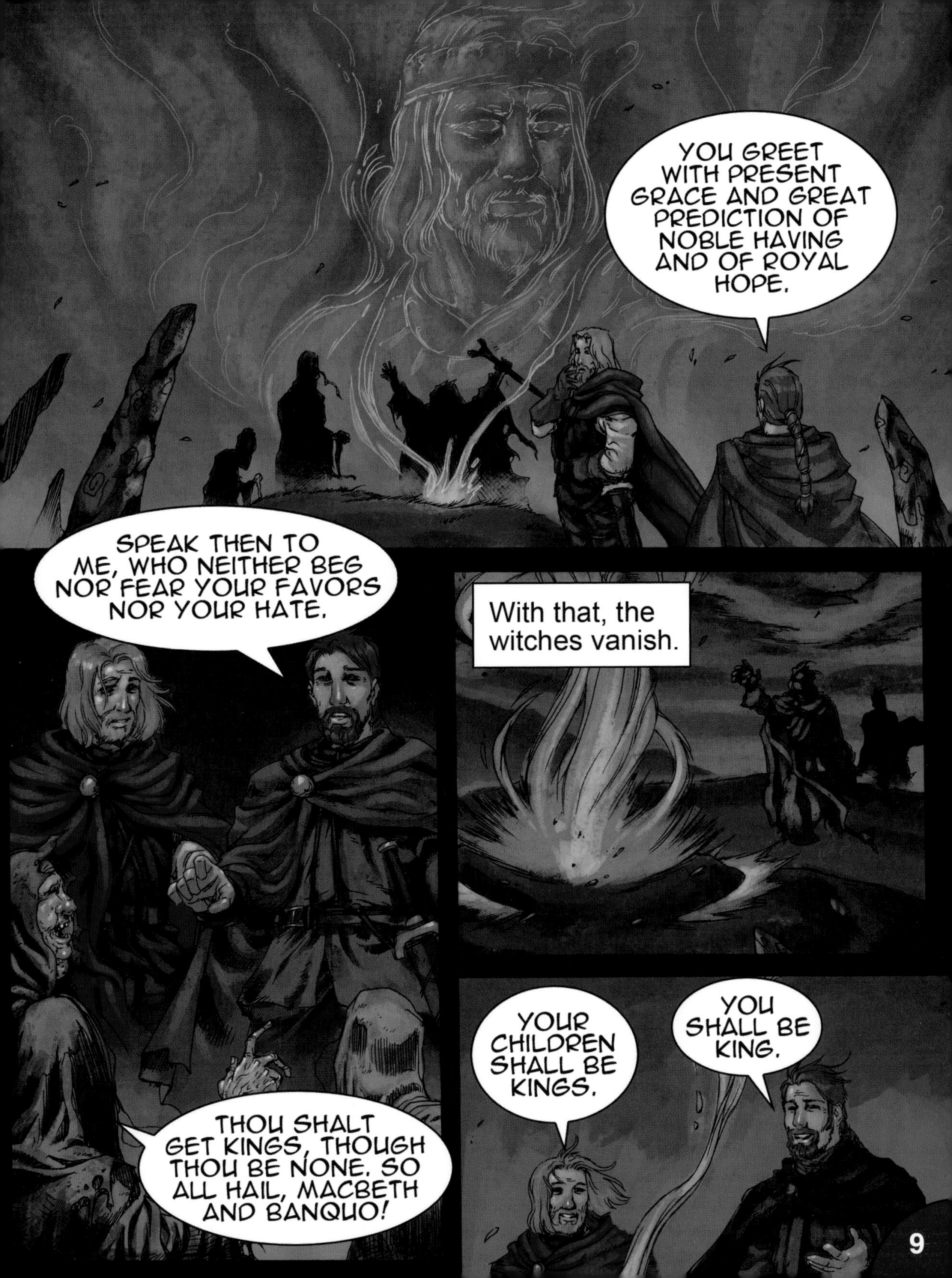
YOU GREET WITH PRESENT GRACE AND GREAT PREDICTION OF NOBLE HAVING AND OF ROYAL HOPE.
SPEAK THEN TO ME, WHO NEITHER BEG NOR FEAR YOUR FAVORS NOR YOUR HATE.
THOU SHALT GET KINGS, THOUGH THOU BE NONE. SO ALL HAIL, MACBETH AND BANQUO!
With that, the witches vanish.
YOU SHALL BE KING.
YOUR CHILDREN SHALL BE KINGS.

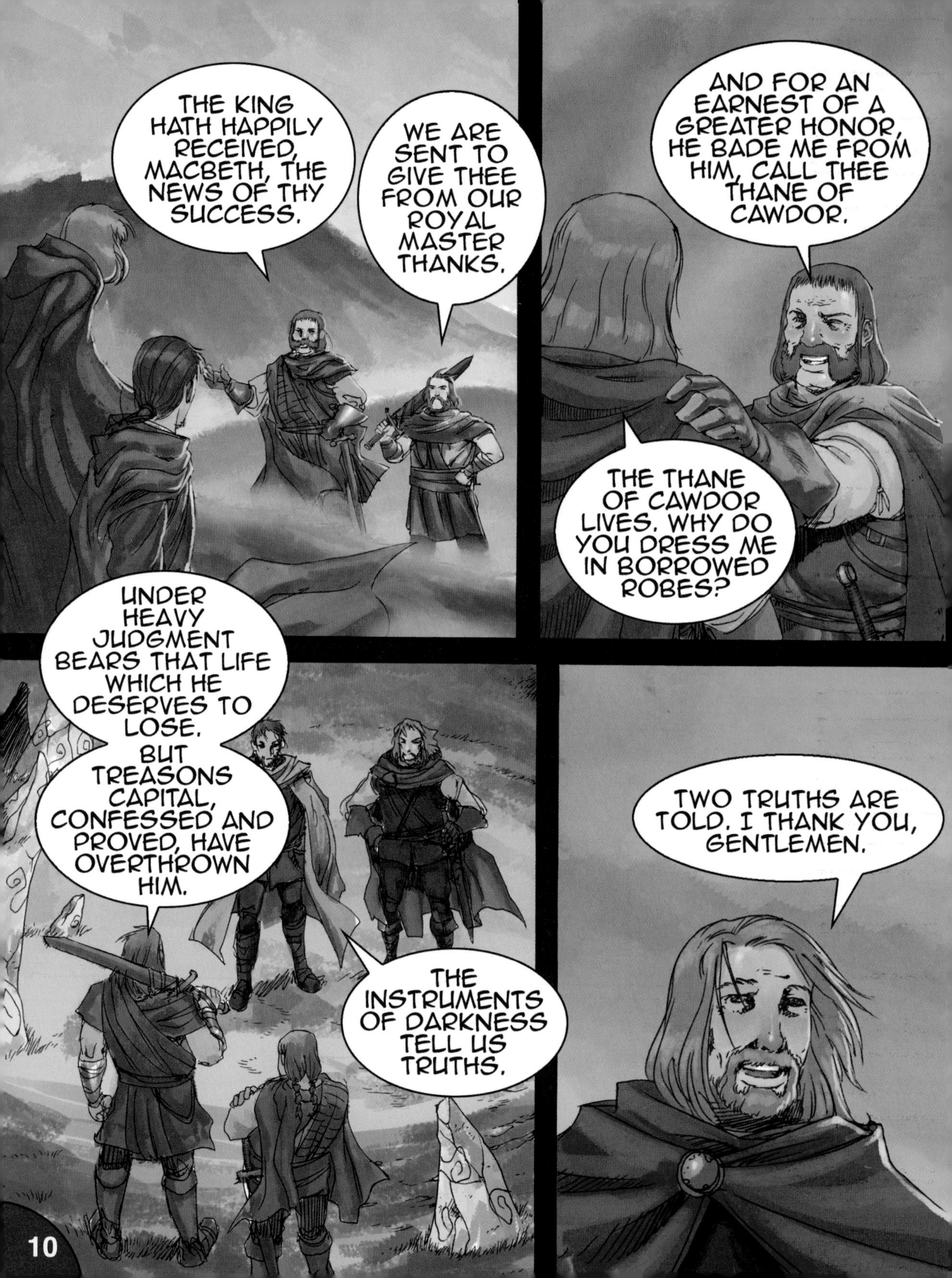
THE KING HATH HAPPILY RECEIVED, MACBETH, THE NEWS OF THY SUCCESS.
WE ARE SENT TO GIVE THEE FROM OUR ROYAL MASTER THANKS.
AND FOR AN EARNEST OF A GREATER HONOR, HE BADE ME FROM HIM, CALL THEE THANE OF CAWDOR.
THE THANE OF CAWDOR LIVES. WHY DO YOU DRESS ME IN BORROWED ROBES?
UNDER HEAVY JUDGMENT BEARS THAT LIFE WHICH HE DESERVES TO LOSE.
BUT TREASONS CAPITAL, CONFESSED AND PROVED, HAVE OVERTHROWN HIM.
THE INSTRUMENTS OF DARKNESS TELL US TRUTHS.
TWO TRUTHS ARE TOLD. I THANK YOU, GENTLEMEN.

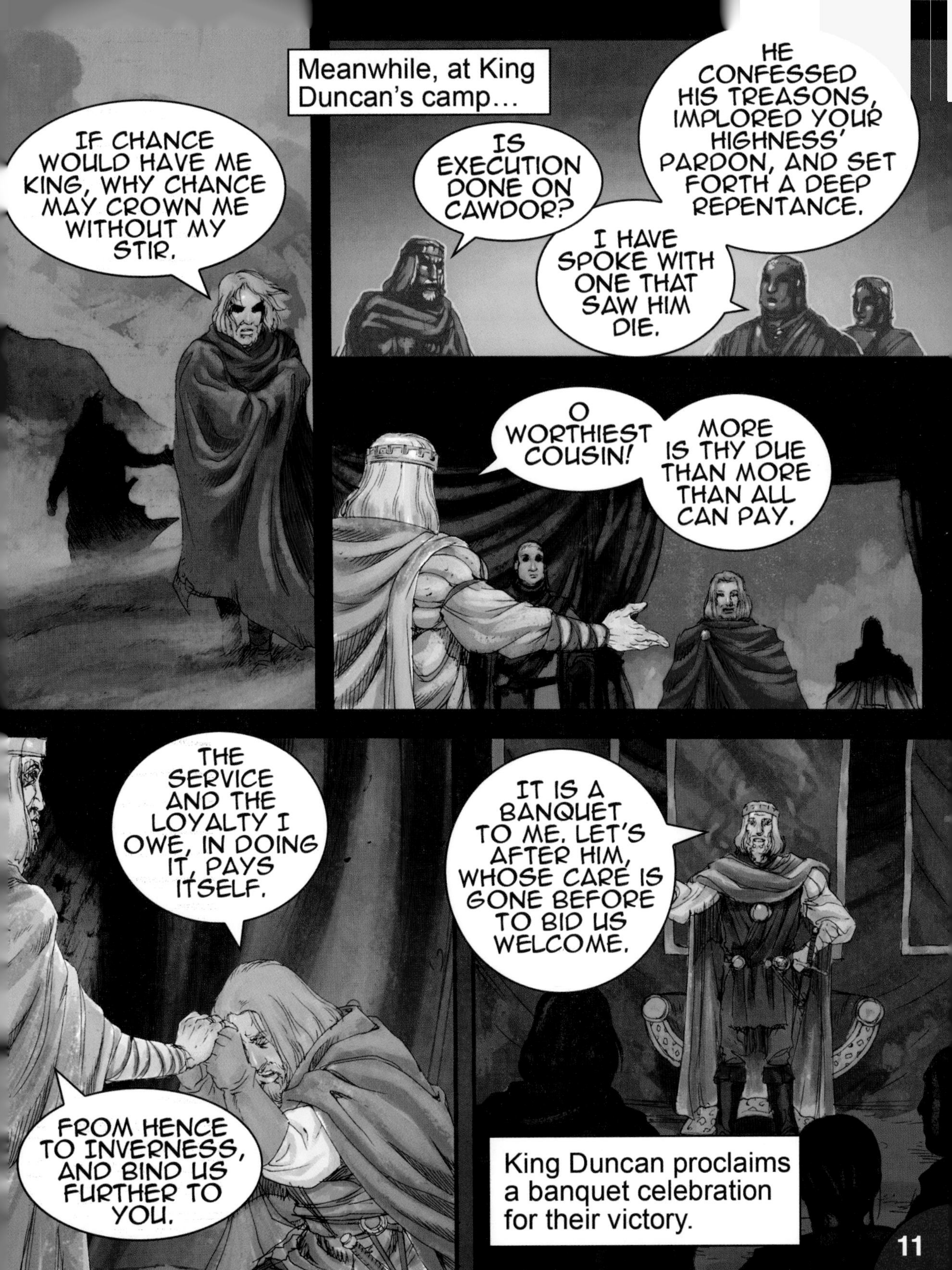
IF CHANCE WOULD HAVE ME KING, WHY CHANCE MAY CROWN ME WITHOUT MY STIR.
Meanwhile, at King Duncan's camp…
IS EXECUTION DONE ON CAWDOR?
HE CONFESSED HIS TREASONS, IMPLORED YOUR HIGHNESS' PARDON, AND SET FORTH A DEEP REPENTANCE.
I HAVE SPOKE WITH ONE THAT SAW HIM DIE.
O WORTHIEST COUSIN!
MORE IS THY DUE THAN MORE THAN ALL CAN PAY.
THE SERVICE AND THE LOYALTY I OWE, IN DOING IT, PAYS ITSELF.
FROM HENCE TO INVERNESS, AND BIND US FURTHER TO YOU.
IT IS A BANQUET TO ME. LET'S AFTER HIM, WHOSE CARE IS GONE BEFORE TO BID US WELCOME.
King Duncan proclaims a banquet celebration for their victory.

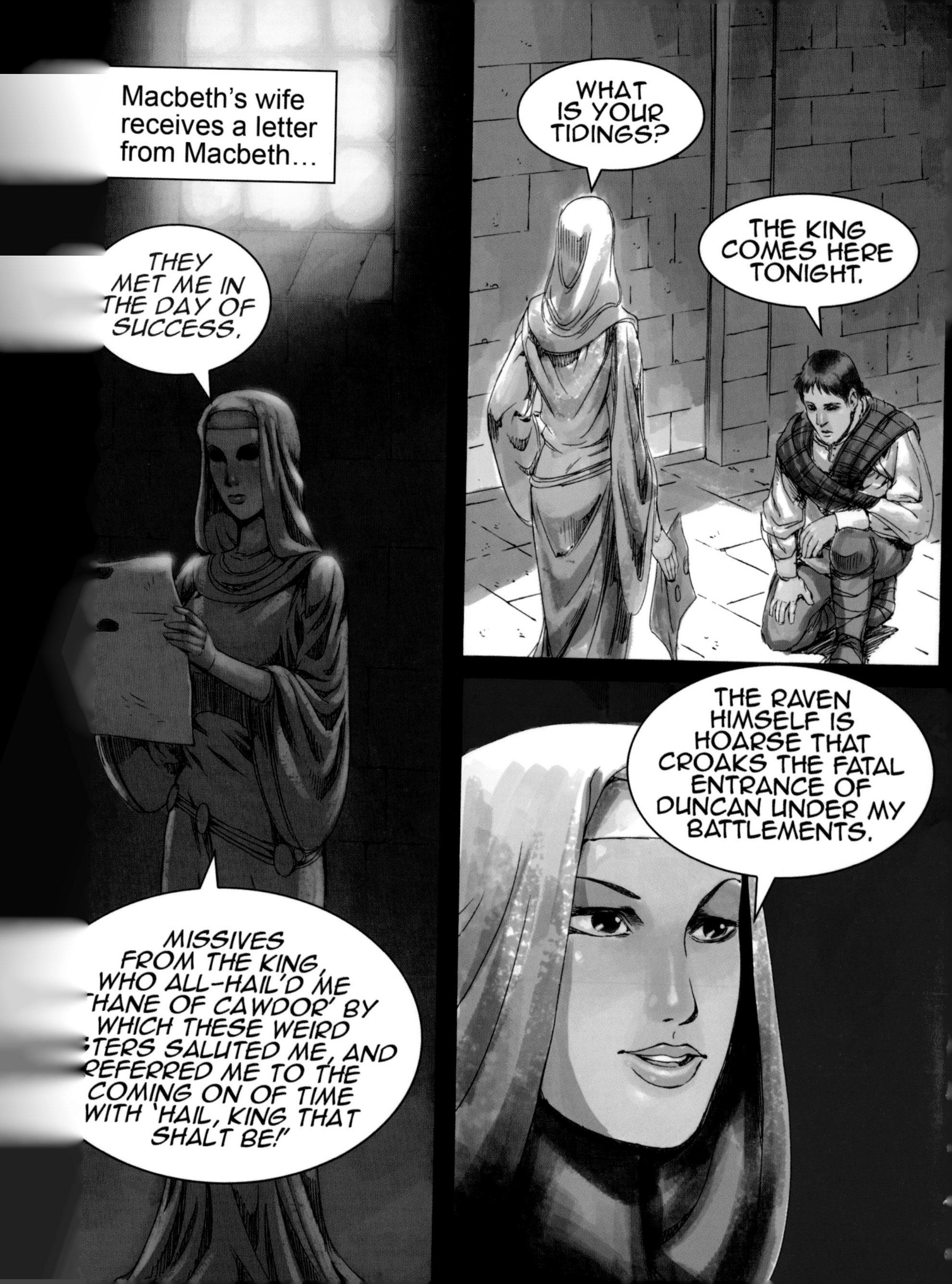

Macbeth's wife receives a letter from Macbeth…
THEY MET ME IN THE DAY OF SUCCESS.
MISSIVES FROM THE KING, WHO ALL-HAIL'D ME 'HANE OF CAWDOR' BY WHICH THESE WEIRD TERS SALUTED ME, AND EFERRED ME TO THE COMING ON OF TIME WITH 'HAIL, KING THAT SHALT BE!'
WHAT IS YOUR TIDINGS?
THE KING COMES HERE TONIGHT.
THE RAVEN HIMSELF IS HOARSE THAT CROAKS THE FATAL ENTRANCE OF DUNCAN UNDER MY BATTLEMENTS.

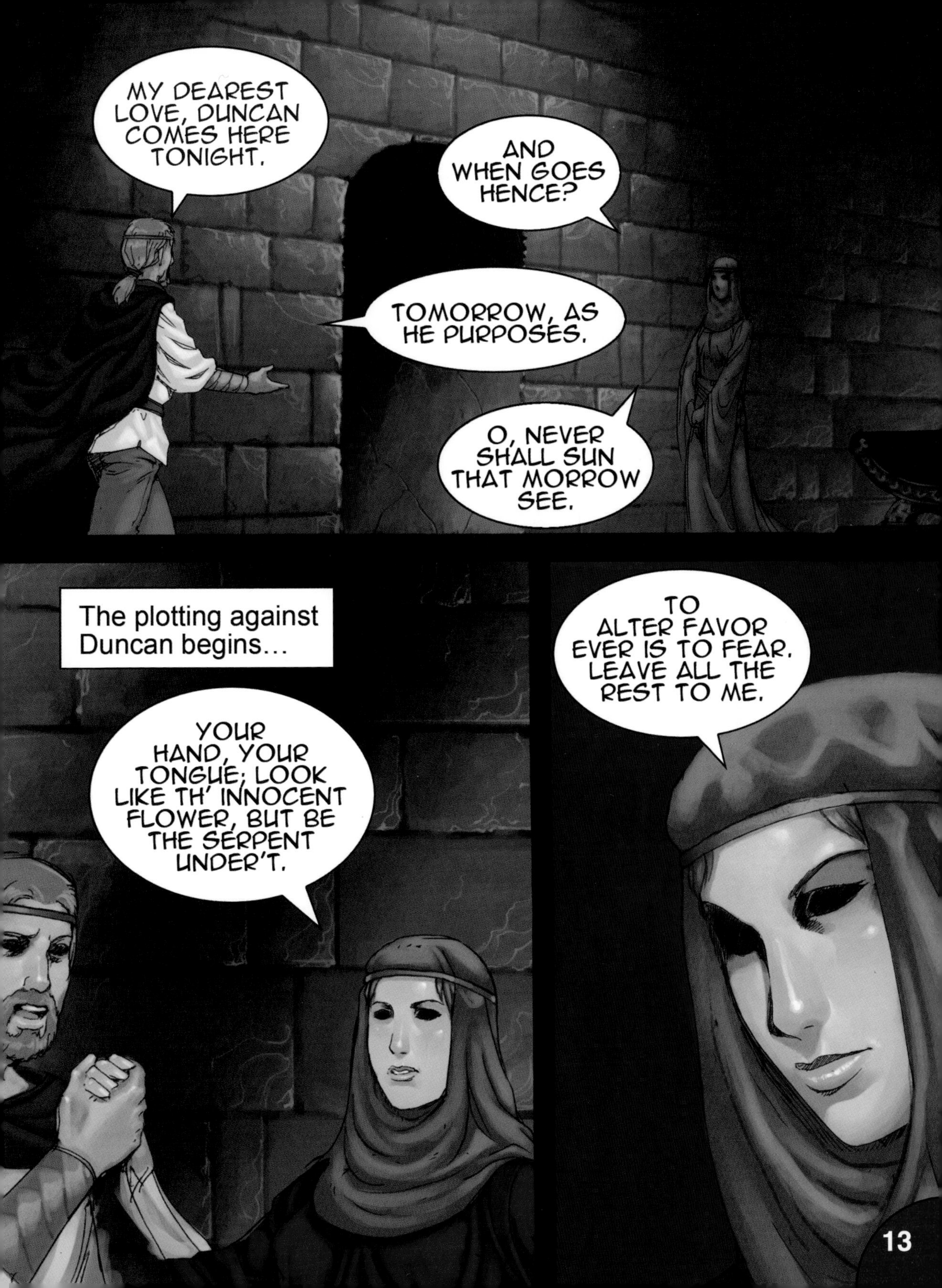
MY DEAREST LOVE, DUNCAN COMES HERE TONIGHT.
AND WHEN GOES HENCE?
TOMORROW, AS HE PURPOSES.
O, NEVER SHALL SUN THAT MORROW SEE.
The plotting against Duncan begins…
YOUR HAND, YOUR TONGUE; LOOK LIKE TH' INNOCENT FLOWER, BUT BE THE SERPENT UNDER'T.
TO ALTER FAVOR EVER IS TO FEAR. LEAVE ALL THE REST TO ME.

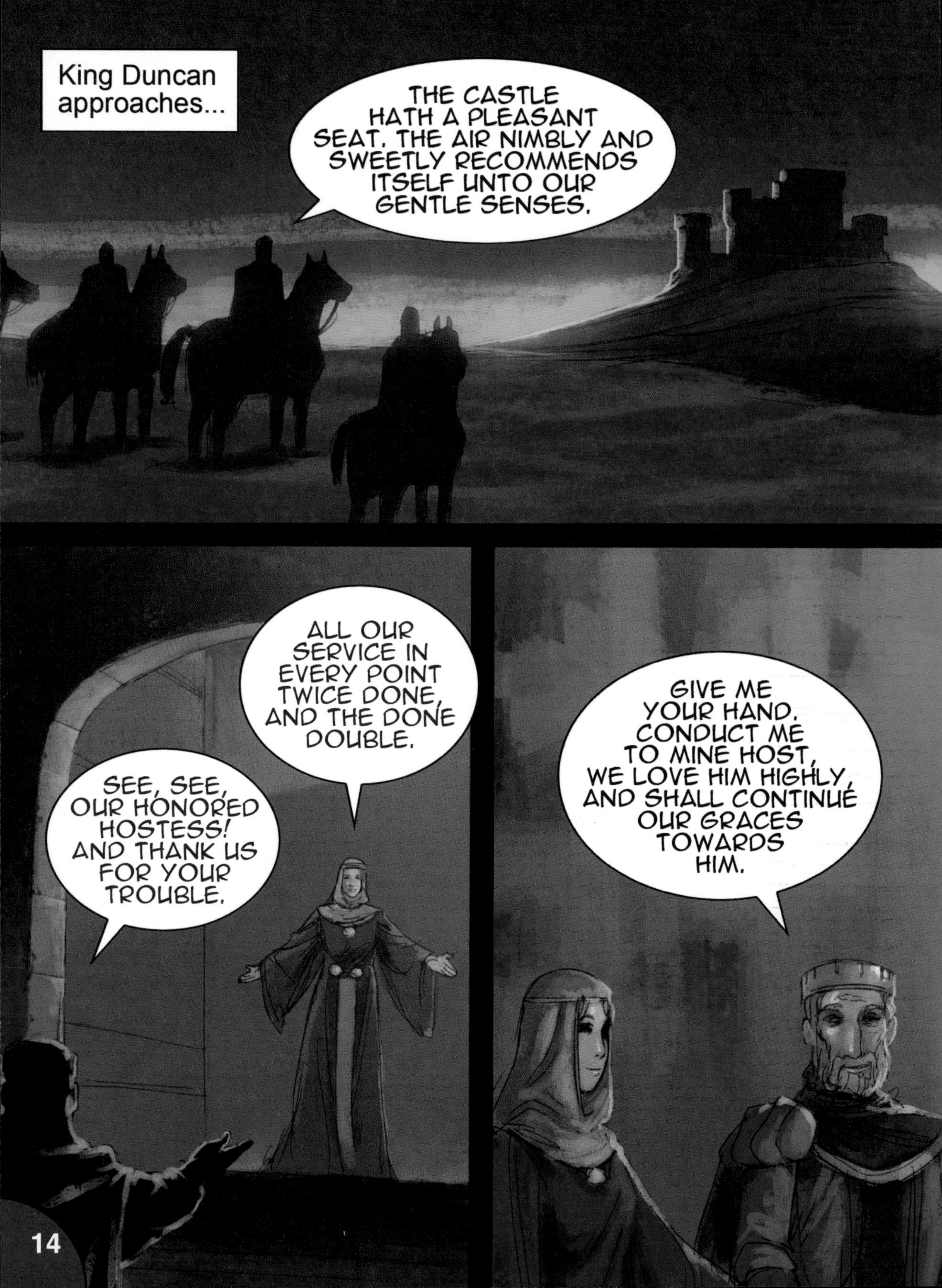
King Duncan approaches...
THE CASTLE HATH A PLEASANT SEAT. THE AIR NIMBLY AND SWEETLY RECOMMENDS ITSELF UNTO OUR GENTLE SENSES.
SEE, SEE, OUR HONORED HOSTESS! AND THANK US FOR YOUR TROUBLE.
ALL OUR SERVICE IN EVERY POINT TWICE DONE, AND THE DONE DOUBLE.
GIVE ME YOUR HAND. CONDUCT ME TO MINE HOST, WE LOVE HIM HIGHLY, AND SHALL CONTINUE OUR GRACES TOWARDS HIM.

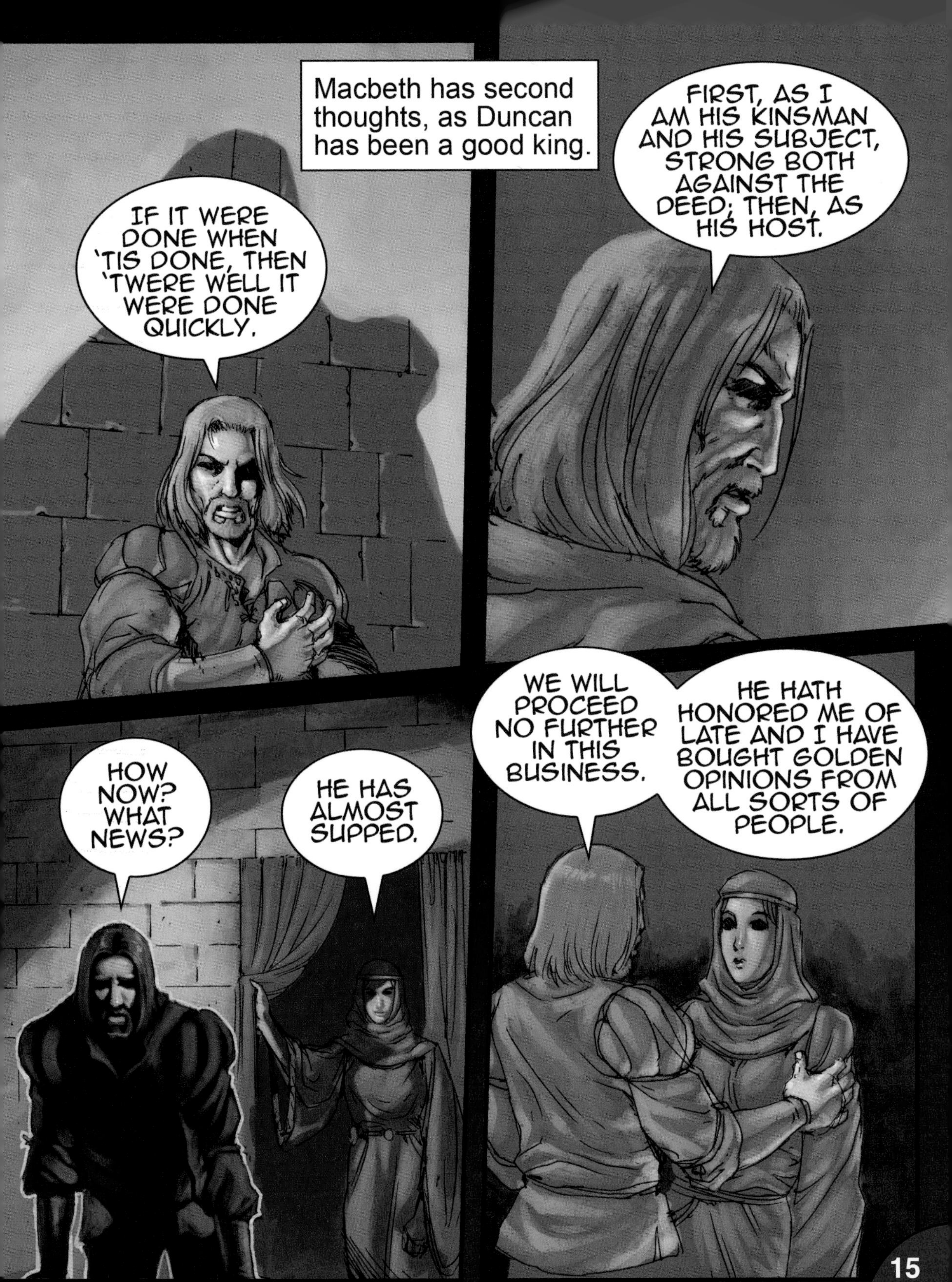
Macbeth has second thoughts, as Duncan has been a good king.
IF IT WERE DONE WHEN 'TIS DONE, THEN 'TWERE WELL IT WERE DONE QUICKLY.
FIRST, AS I AM HIS KINSMAN AND HIS SUBJECT, STRONG BOTH AGAINST THE DEED; THEN, AS HIS HOST.
HOW NOW? WHAT NEWS?
HE HAS ALMOST SUPPED.
WE WILL PROCEED NO FURTHER IN THIS BUSINESS.
HE HATH HONORED ME OF LATE AND I HAVE BOUGHT GOLDEN OPINIONS FROM ALL SORTS OF PEOPLE.

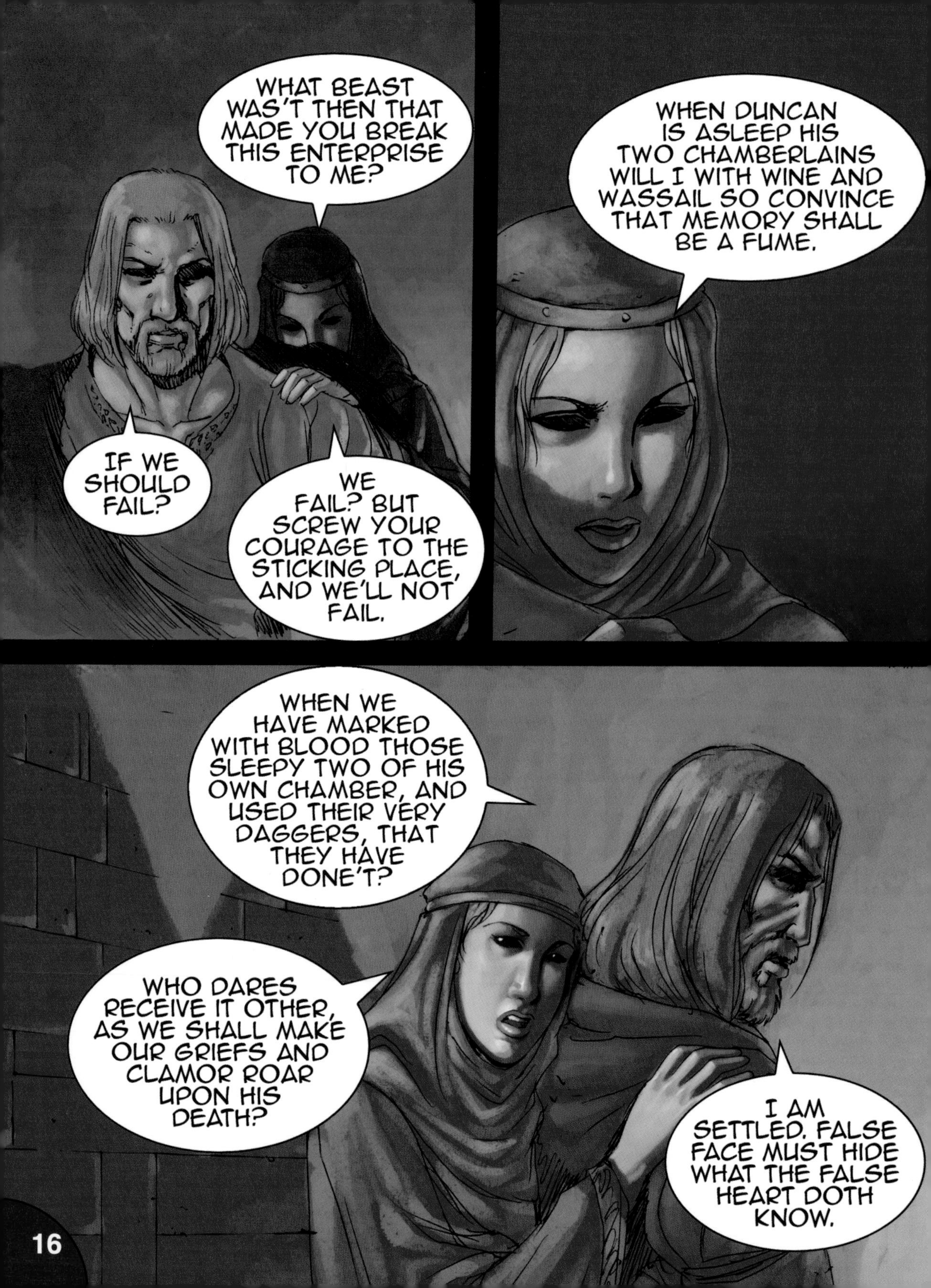
WHAT BEAST WAS'T THEN THAT MADE YOU BREAK THIS ENTERPRISE TO ME?
IF WE SHOULD FAIL?
WE FAIL? BUT SCREW YOUR COURAGE TO THE STICKING PLACE, AND WE'LL NOT FAIL.
WHEN DUNCAN IS ASLEEP HIS TWO CHAMBERLAINS WILL I WITH WINE AND WASSAIL SO CONVINCE THAT MEMORY SHALL BE A FUME.
WHEN WE HAVE MARKED WITH BLOOD THOSE SLEEPY TWO OF HIS OWN CHAMBER, AND USED THEIR VERY DAGGERS, THAT THEY HAVE DONE'T?
WHO DARES RECEIVE IT OTHER, AS WE SHALL MAKE OUR GRIEFS AND CLAMOR ROAR UPON HIS DEATH?
I AM SETTLED. FALSE FACE MUST HIDE WHAT THE FALSE HEART DOTH KNOW.

Act II

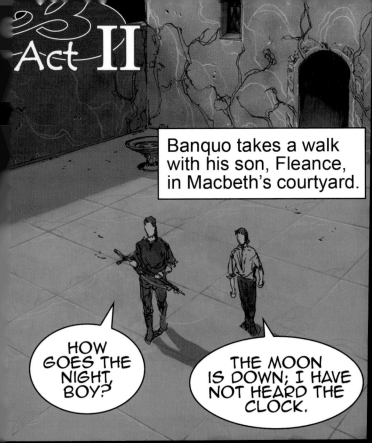

Banquo takes a walk with his son, Fleance, in Macbeth's courtyard.

HOW GOES THE NIGHT, BOY?

THE MOON IS DOWN; I HAVE NOT HEARD THE CLOCK.

HOLD, TAKE MY SWORD. THEIR CANDLES ARE ALL OUT.

WHO'S THERE?

A FRIEND.

WHAT, SIR, NOT YET AT REST?

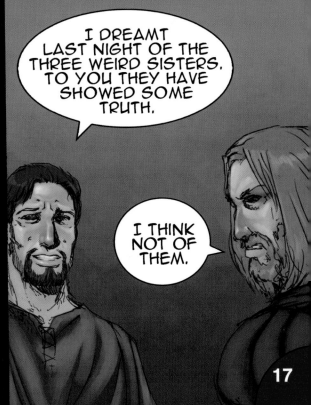

I DREAMT LAST NIGHT OF THE THREE WEIRD SISTERS. TO YOU THEY HAVE SHOWED SOME TRUTH.

I THINK NOT OF THEM.

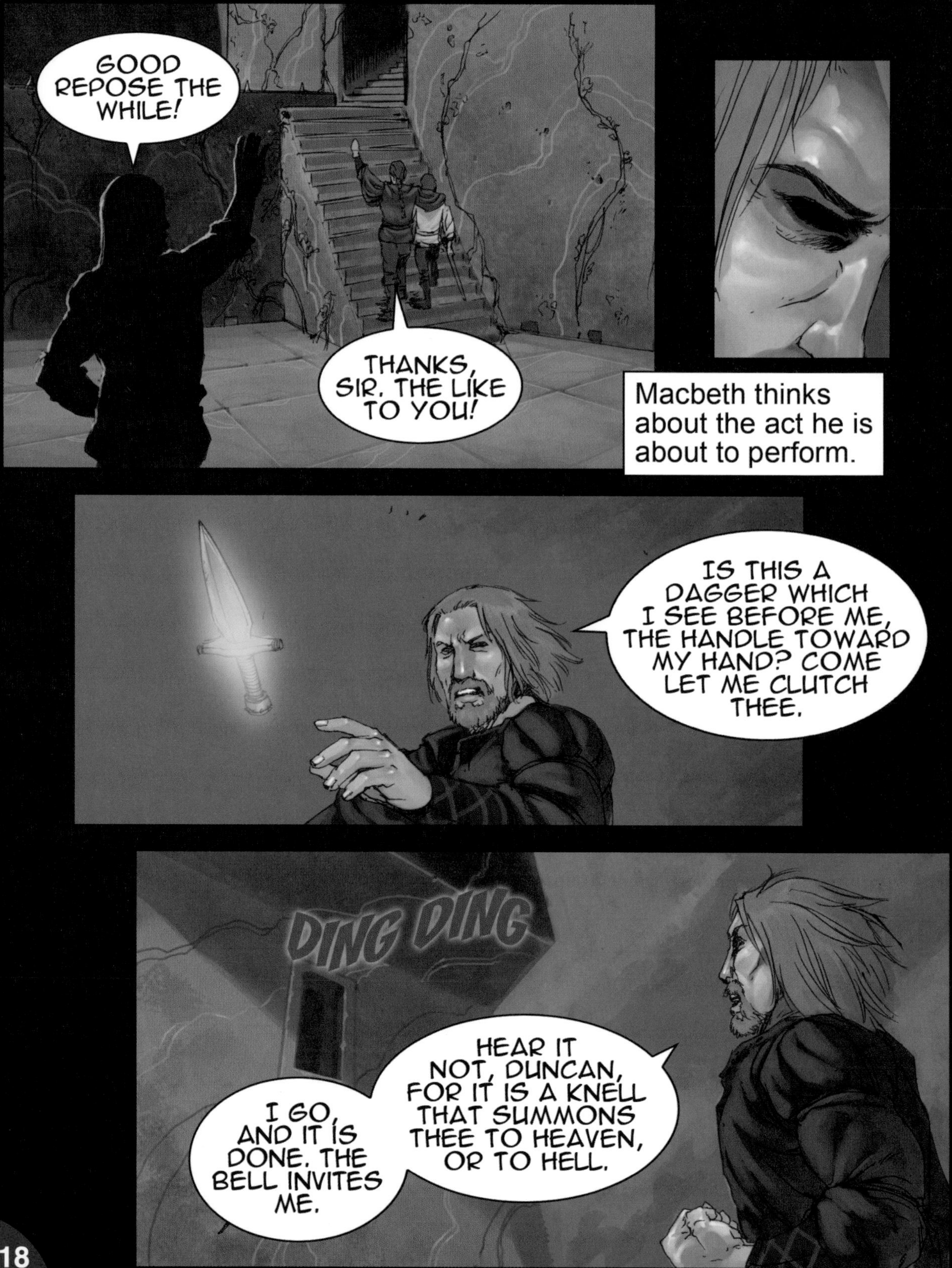
GOOD REPOSE THE WHILE!
THANKS, SIR. THE LIKE TO YOU!
Macbeth thinks about the act he is about to perform.
IS THIS A DAGGER WHICH I SEE BEFORE ME, THE HANDLE TOWARD MY HAND? COME LET ME CLUTCH THEE.
DING DING
I GO, AND IT IS DONE. THE BELL INVITES ME.
HEAR IT NOT, DUNCAN, FOR IT IS A KNELL THAT SUMMONS THEE TO HEAVEN, OR TO HELL.

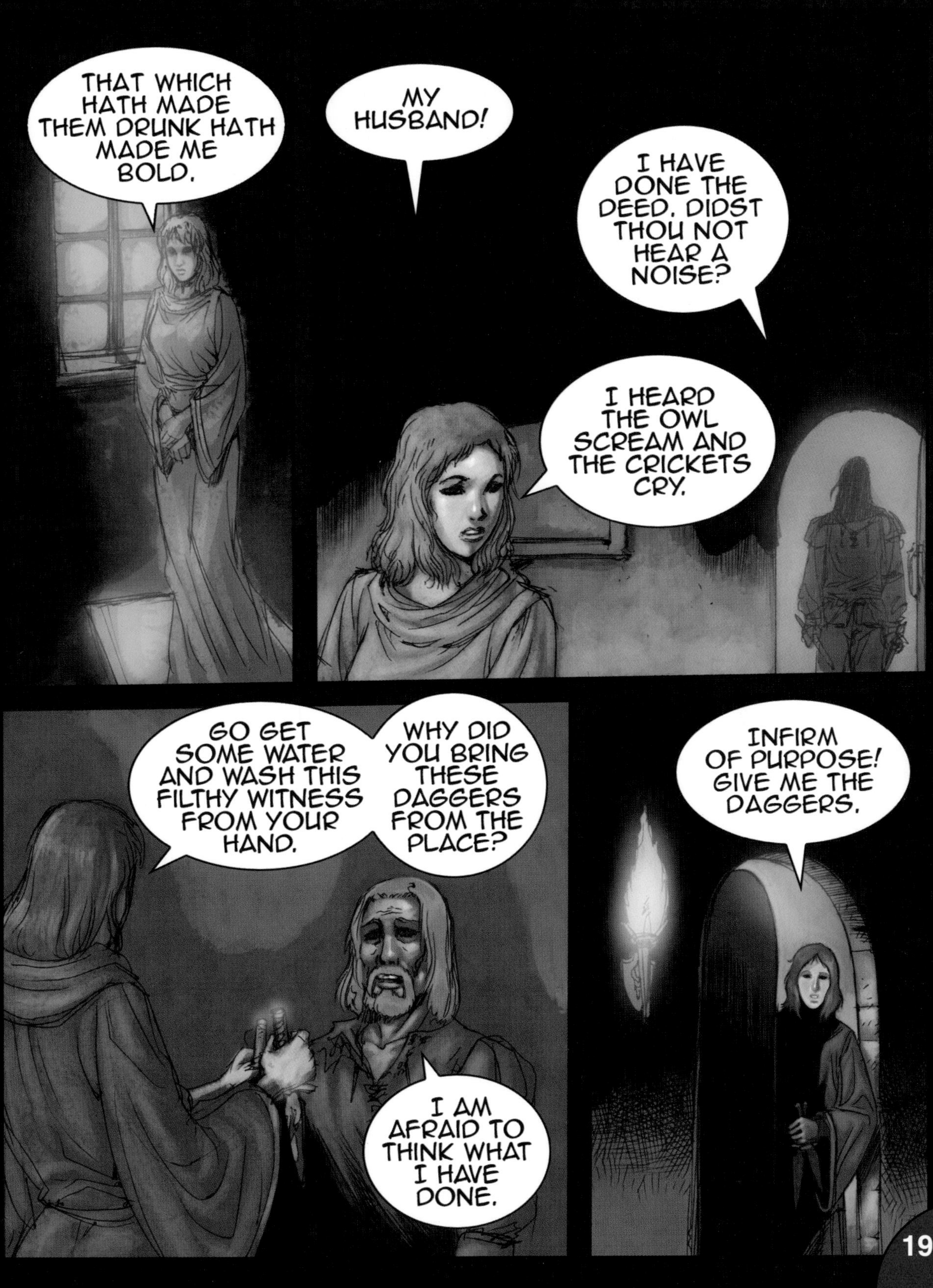
THAT WHICH HATH MADE THEM DRUNK HATH MADE ME BOLD.
MY HUSBAND!
I HAVE DONE THE DEED. DIDST THOU NOT HEAR A NOISE?
I HEARD THE OWL SCREAM AND THE CRICKETS CRY.
GO GET SOME WATER AND WASH THIS FILTHY WITNESS FROM YOUR HAND.
WHY DID YOU BRING THESE DAGGERS FROM THE PLACE?
I AM AFRAID TO THINK WHAT I HAVE DONE.
INFIRM OF PURPOSE! GIVE ME THE DAGGERS.

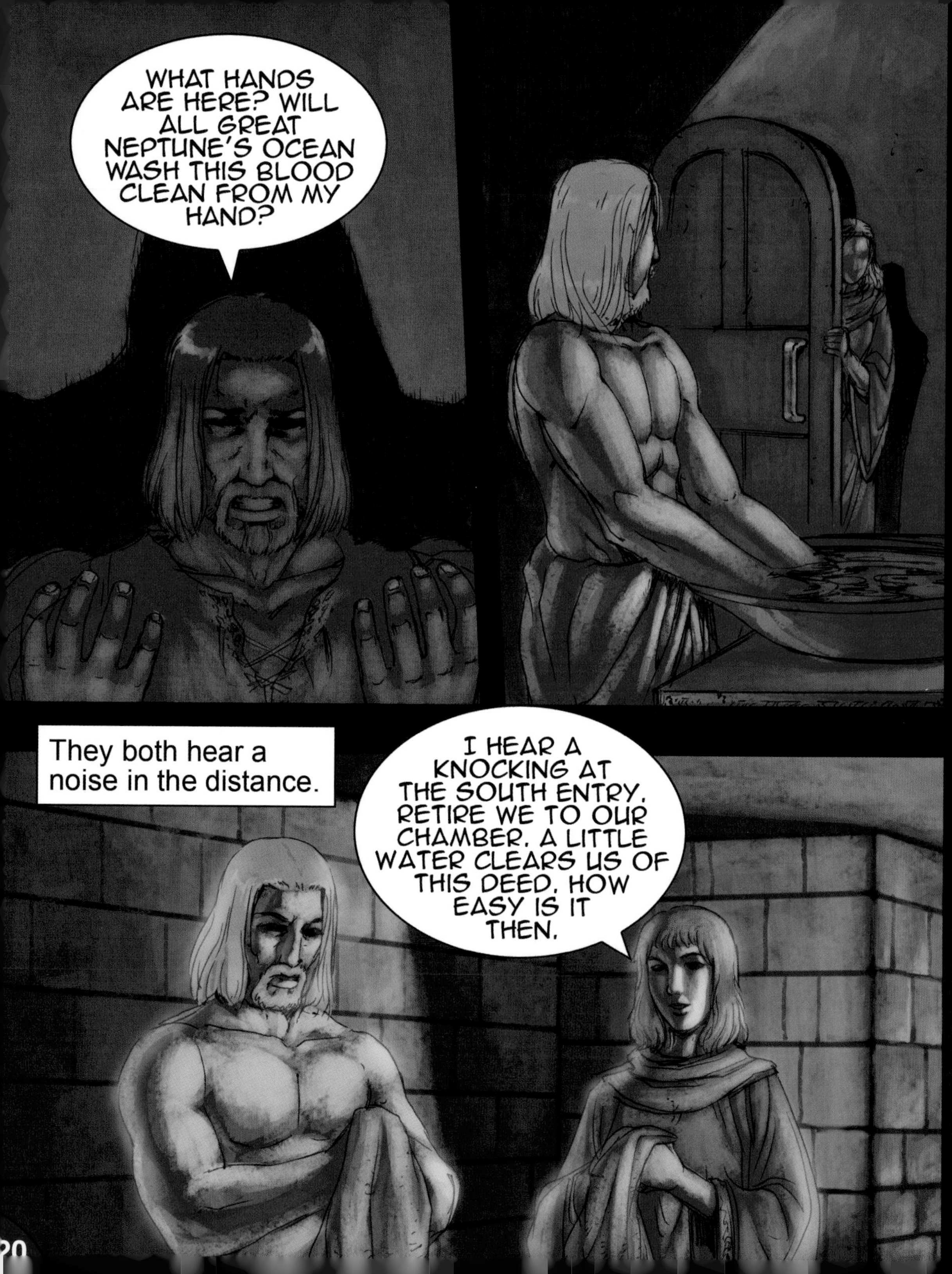
WHAT HANDS ARE HERE? WILL ALL GREAT NEPTUNE'S OCEAN WASH THIS BLOOD CLEAN FROM MY HAND?
They both hear a noise in the distance.
I HEAR A KNOCKING AT THE SOUTH ENTRY. RETIRE WE TO OUR CHAMBER. A LITTLE WATER CLEARS US OF THIS DEED. HOW EASY IS IT THEN.

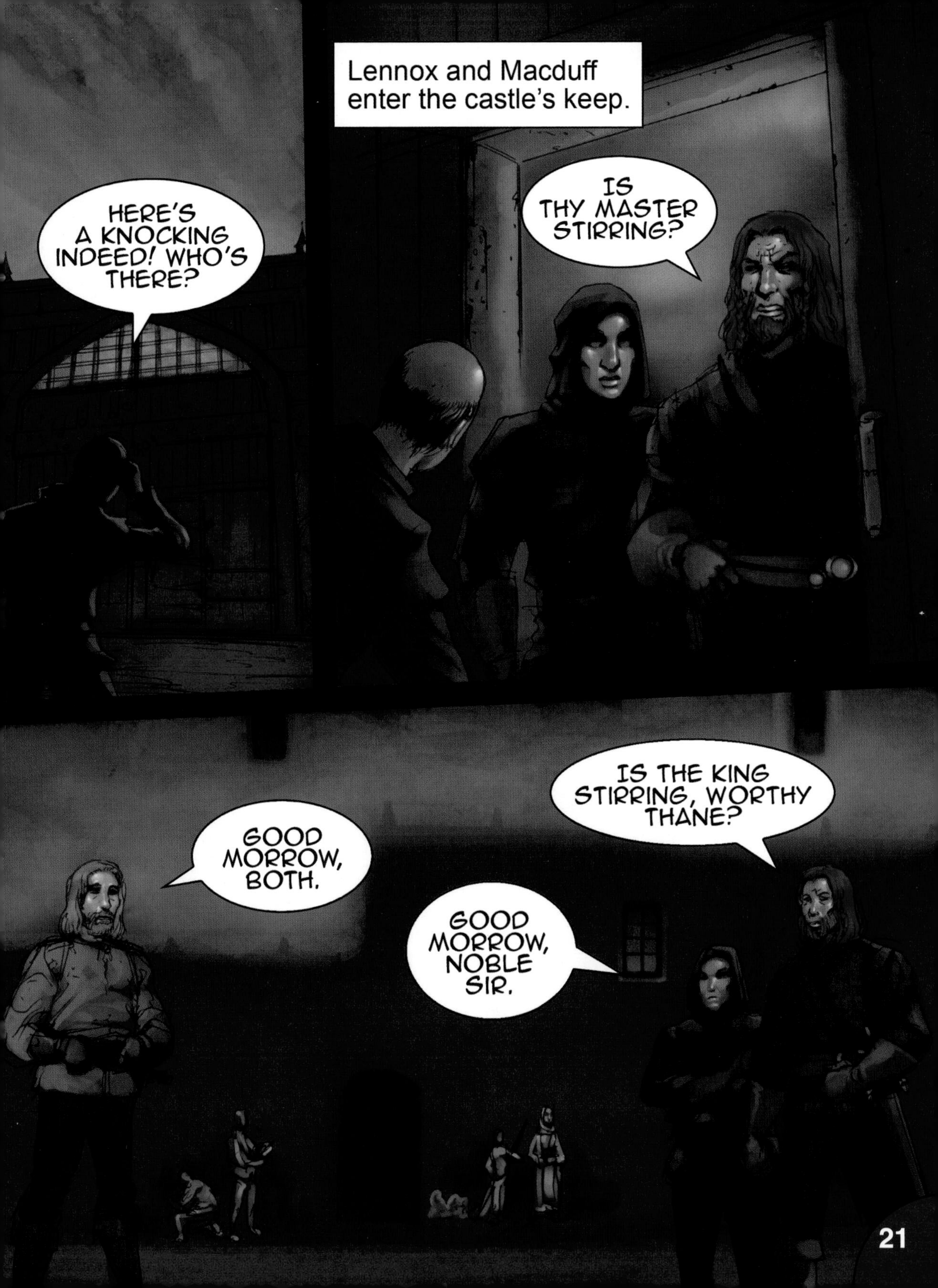
Lennox and Macduff enter the castle's keep.
HERE'S A KNOCKING INDEED! WHO'S THERE?
IS THY MASTER STIRRING?
GOOD MORROW, BOTH.
IS THE KING STIRRING, WORTHY THANE?
GOOD MORROW, NOBLE SIR.

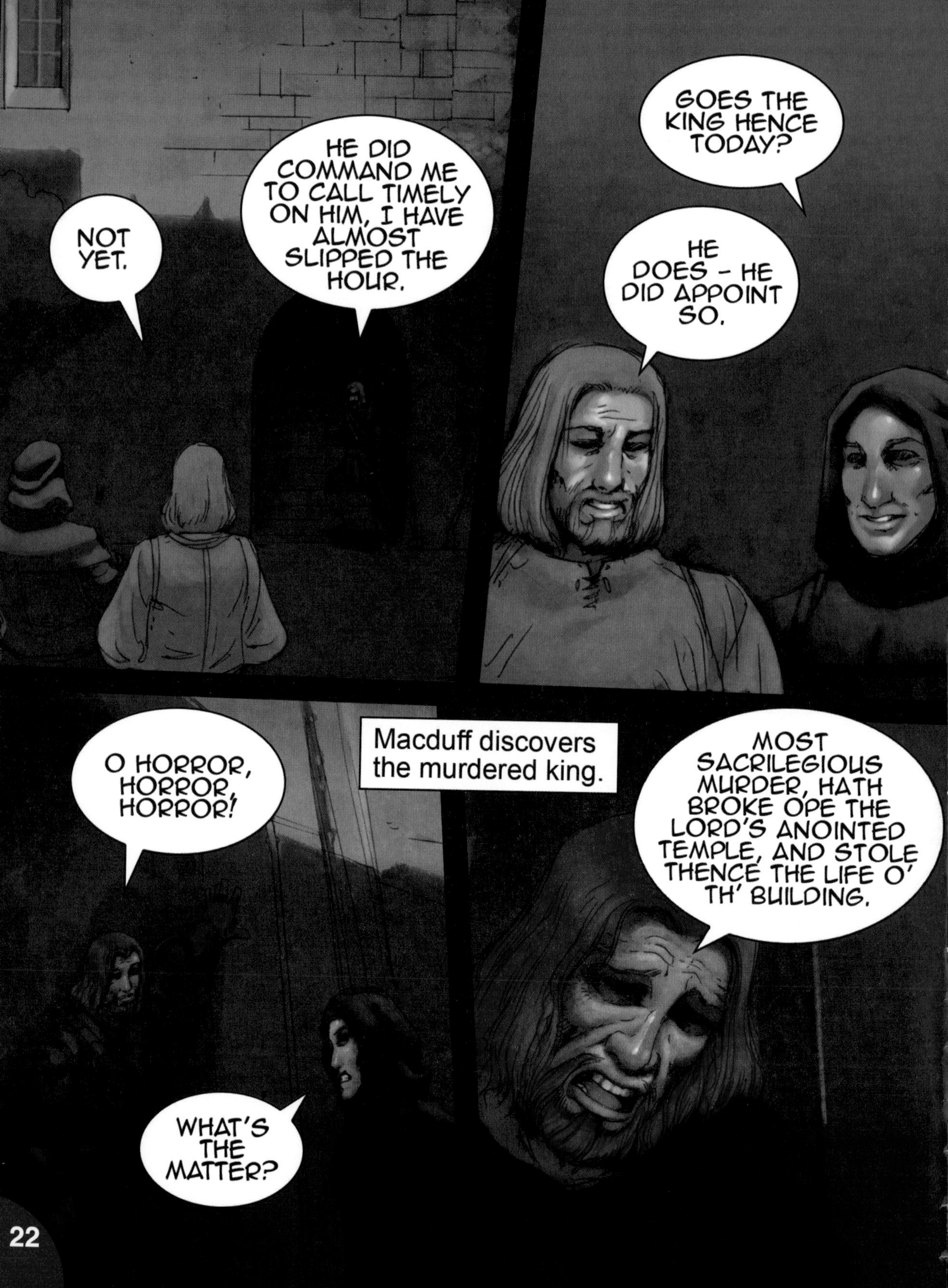
HE DID COMMAND ME TO CALL TIMELY ON HIM, I HAVE ALMOST SLIPPED THE HOUR.
NOT YET.
GOES THE KING HENCE TODAY?
HE DOES - HE DID APPOINT SO.
Macduff discovers the murdered king.
O HORROR, HORROR, HORROR!
WHAT'S THE MATTER?
MOST SACRILEGIOUS MURDER, HATH BROKE OPE THE LORD'S ANOINTED TEMPLE, AND STOLE THENCE THE LIFE O' TH' BUILDING.

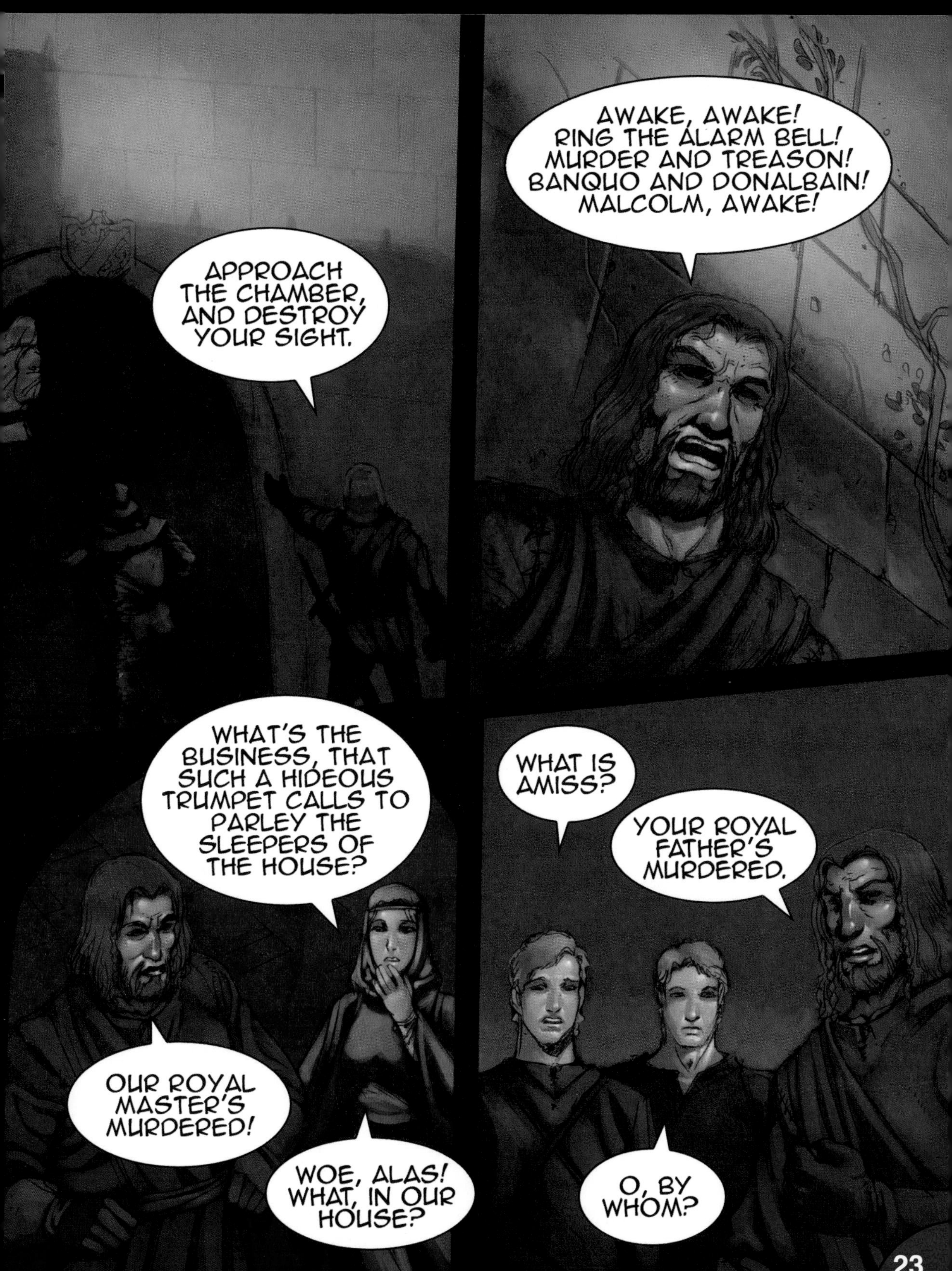
APPROACH THE CHAMBER, AND DESTROY YOUR SIGHT.
AWAKE, AWAKE! RING THE ALARM BELL! MURDER AND TREASON! BANQUO AND DONALBAIN! MALCOLM, AWAKE!
WHAT'S THE BUSINESS, THAT SUCH A HIDEOUS TRUMPET CALLS TO PARLEY THE SLEEPERS OF THE HOUSE?
OUR ROYAL MASTER'S MURDERED!
WOE, ALAS! WHAT, IN OUR HOUSE?
WHAT IS AMISS?
YOUR ROYAL FATHER'S MURDERED.
O, BY WHOM?

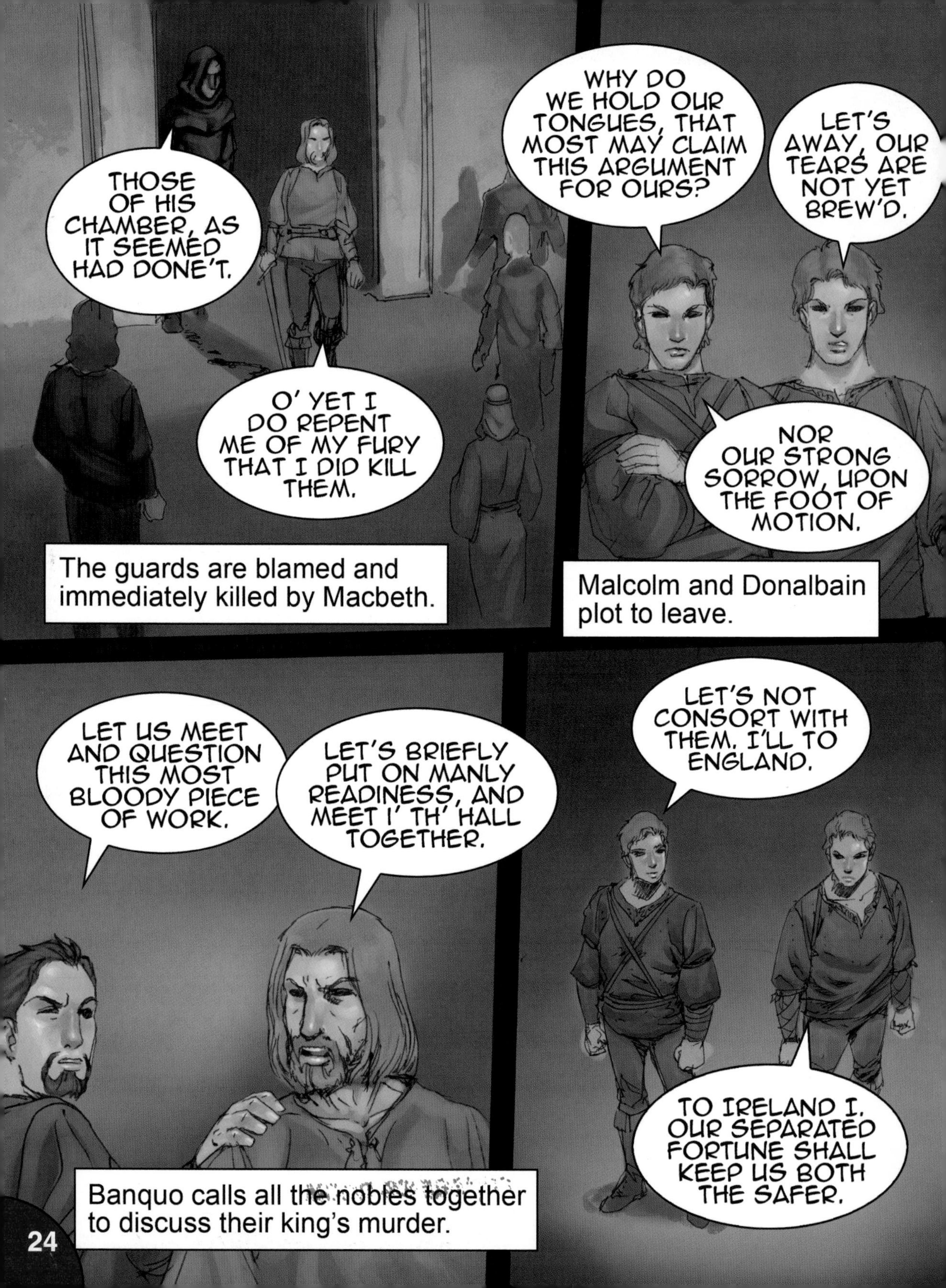
THOSE OF HIS CHAMBER, AS IT SEEMED HAD DONE'T.
O' YET I DO REPENT ME OF MY FURY THAT I DID KILL THEM.
The guards are blamed and immediately killed by Macbeth.
WHY DO WE HOLD OUR TONGUES, THAT MOST MAY CLAIM THIS ARGUMENT FOR OURS?
LET'S AWAY, OUR TEARS ARE NOT YET BREW'D.
NOR OUR STRONG SORROW, UPON THE FOOT OF MOTION.
Malcolm and Donalbain plot to leave.
LET US MEET AND QUESTION THIS MOST BLOODY PIECE OF WORK.
LET'S BRIEFLY PUT ON MANLY READINESS, AND MEET I' TH' HALL TOGETHER.
Banquo calls all the nobles together to discuss their king's murder.
LET'S NOT CONSORT WITH THEM. I'LL TO ENGLAND.
TO IRELAND I. OUR SEPARATED FORTUNE SHALL KEEP US BOTH THE SAFER.

IS'T KNOWN WHO DID THIS MORE THAN BLOODY DEED?

Outside the castle, people also discuss the murder.

THOSE THAT MACBETH HATH SLAIN.

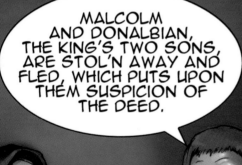

MALCOLM AND DONALBIAN, THE KING'S TWO SONS, ARE STOL'N AWAY AND FLED, WHICH PUTS UPON THEM SUSPICION OF THE DEED.

THE SOVEREIGNTY WILL FALL UPON MACBETH.

HE IS ALREADY NAMED, AND GONE TO SCONE.

WHERE IS DUNCAN'S BODY?

CARRIED TO COLMEKILL.

WILL YOU GO TO SCONE?

NO, COUSIN, I'LL TO FIFE.

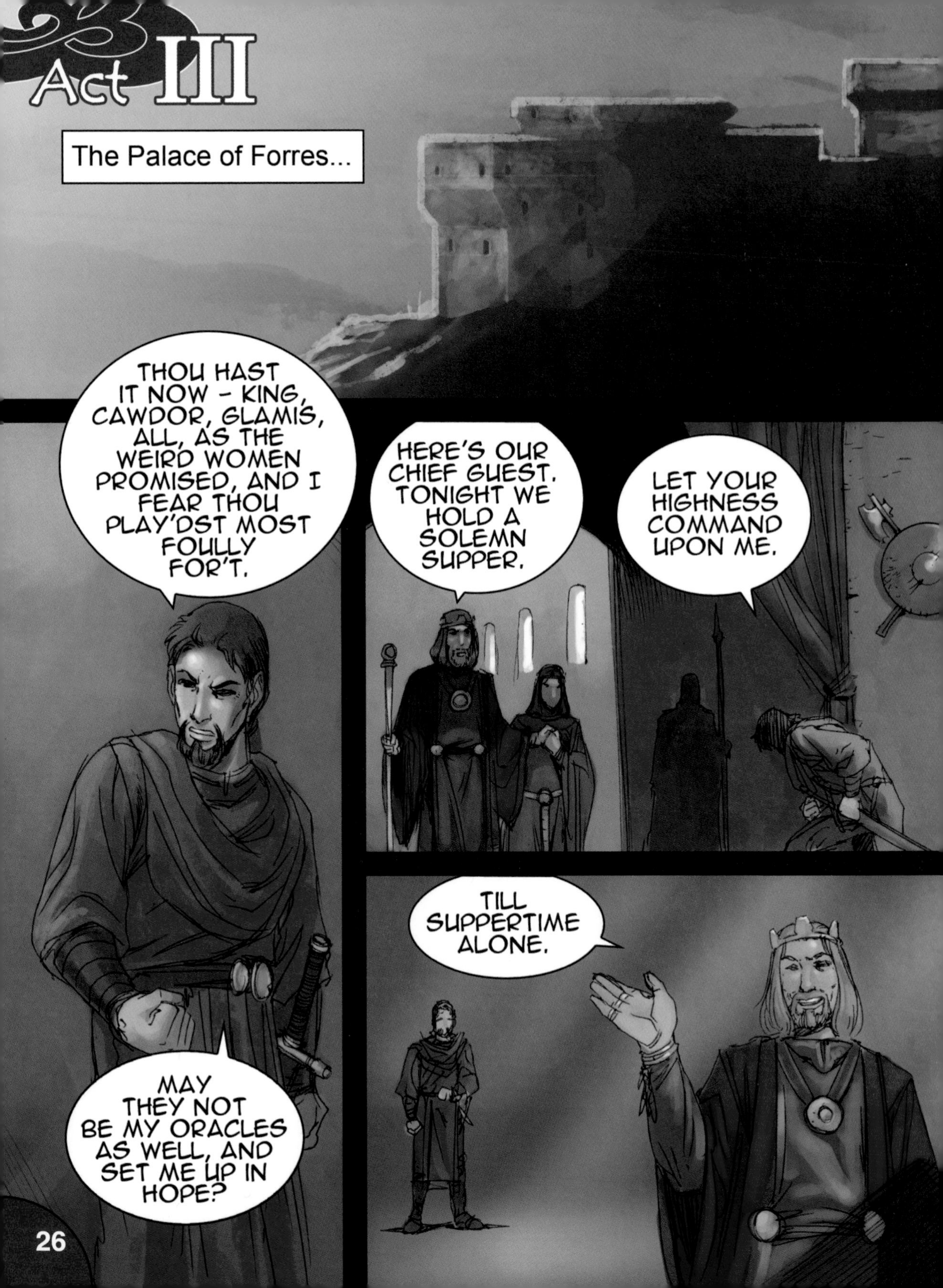
Act III
The Palace of Forres...
THOU HAST IT NOW - KING, CAWDOR, GLAMIS, ALL, AS THE WEIRD WOMEN PROMISED, AND I FEAR THOU PLAY'DST MOST FOULLY FOR'T.
MAY THEY NOT BE MY ORACLES AS WELL, AND SET ME UP IN HOPE?
HERE'S OUR CHIEF GUEST. TONIGHT WE HOLD A SOLEMN SUPPER.
LET YOUR HIGHNESS COMMAND UPON ME.
TILL SUPPERTIME ALONE.

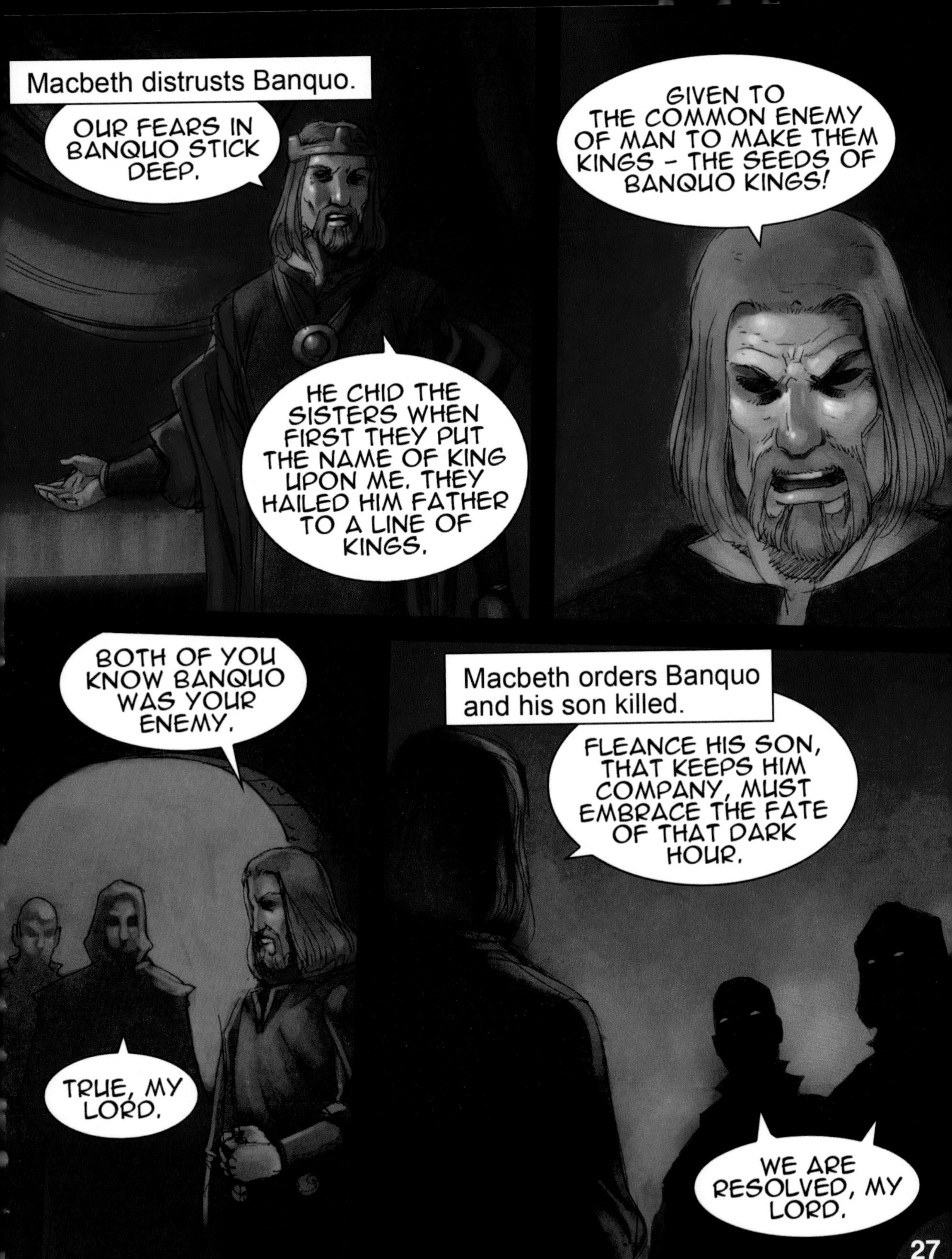

Macbeth distrusts Banquo.
OUR FEARS IN BANQUO STICK DEEP.
HE CHID THE SISTERS WHEN FIRST THEY PUT THE NAME OF KING UPON ME. THEY HAILED HIM FATHER TO A LINE OF KINGS.
GIVEN TO THE COMMON ENEMY OF MAN TO MAKE THEM KINGS - THE SEEDS OF BANQUO KINGS!
BOTH OF YOU KNOW BANQUO WAS YOUR ENEMY.
TRUE, MY LORD.
Macbeth orders Banquo and his son killed.
FLEANCE HIS SON, THAT KEEPS HIM COMPANY, MUST EMBRACE THE FATE OF THAT DARK HOUR.
WE ARE RESOLVED, MY LORD.

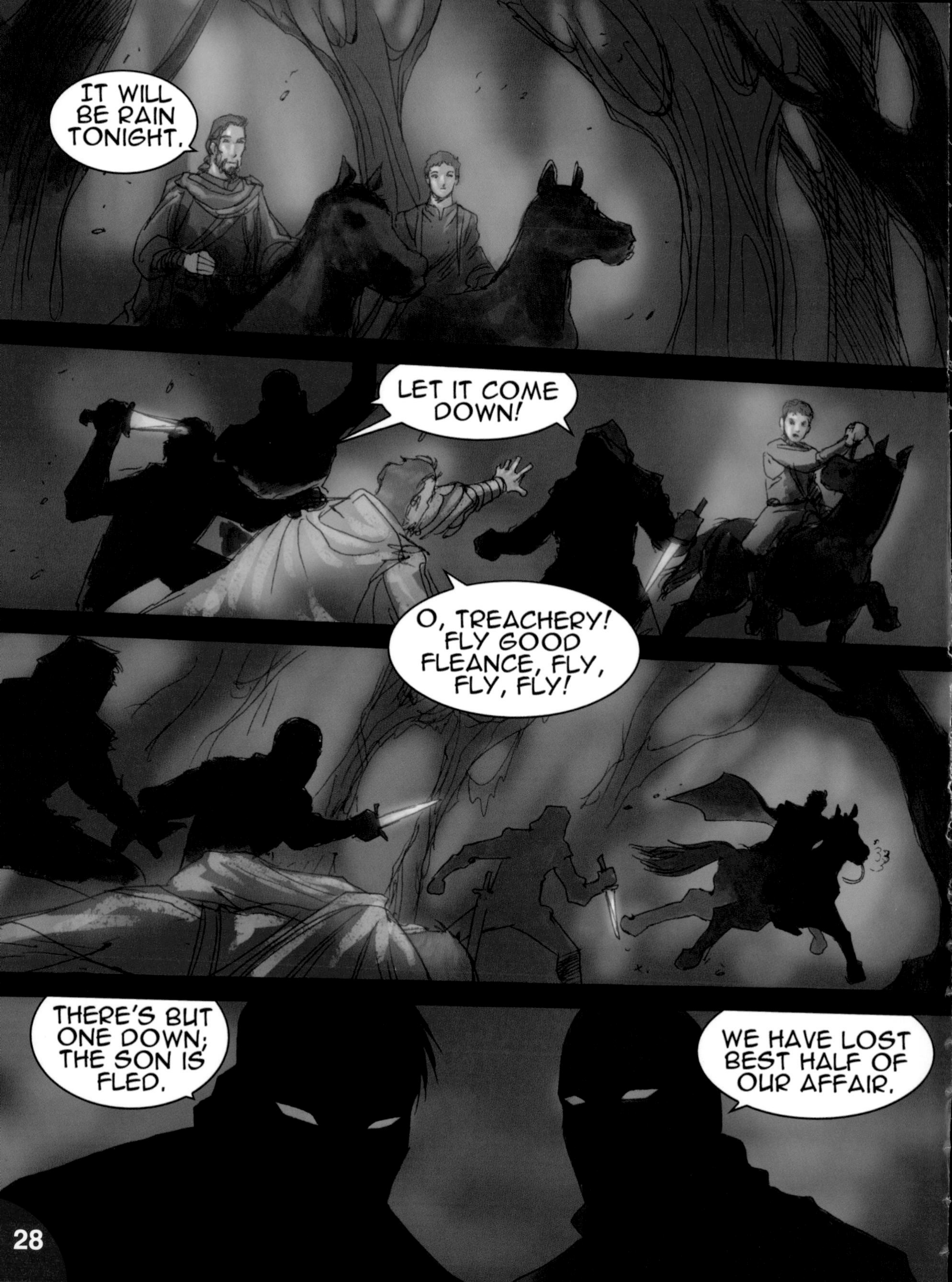
IT WILL BE RAIN TONIGHT.
LET IT COME DOWN!
O, TREACHERY! FLY GOOD FLEANCE, FLY, FLY, FLY!
THERE'S BUT ONE DOWN; THE SON IS FLED.
WE HAVE LOST BEST HALF OF OUR AFFAIR.

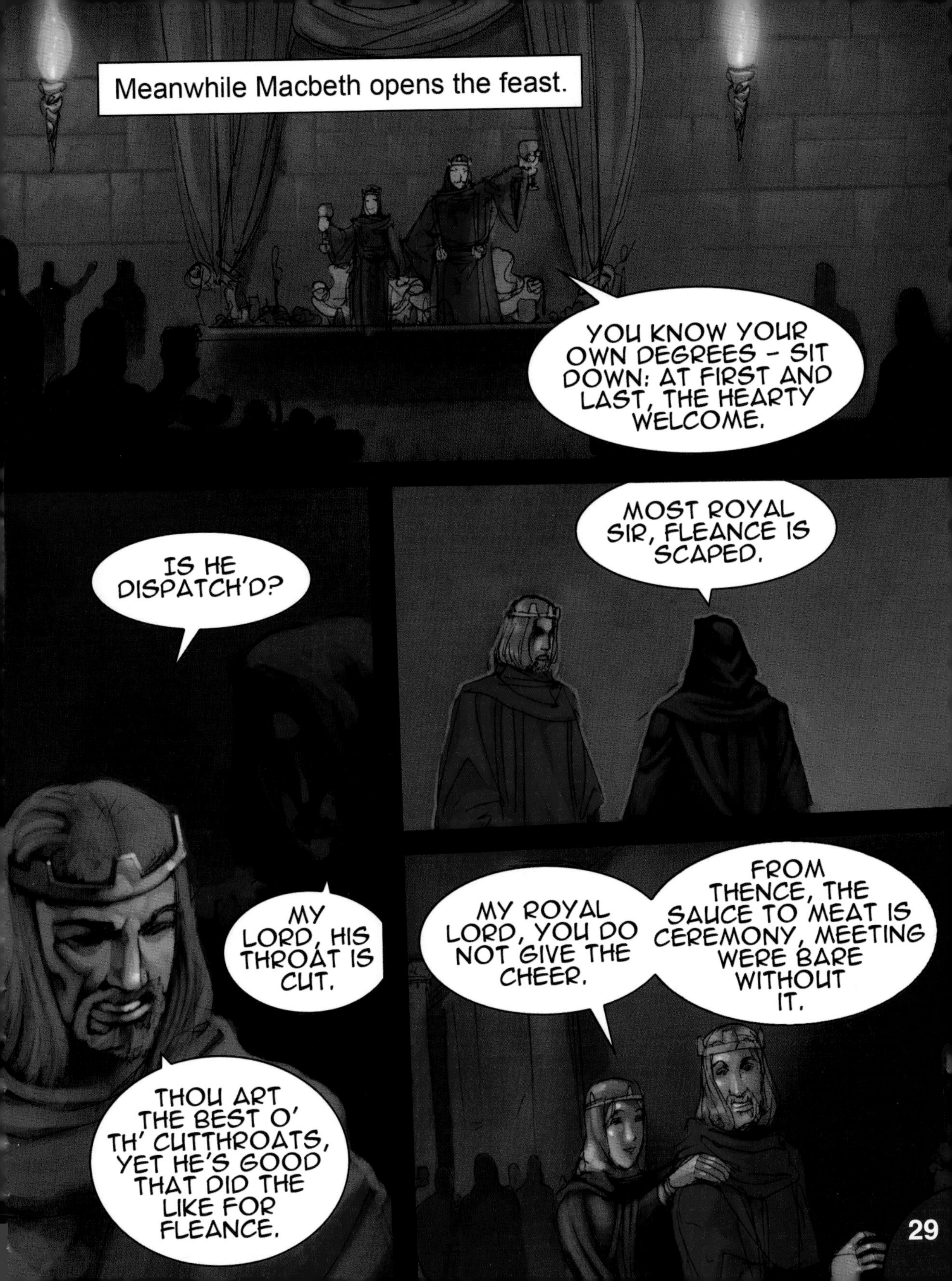

Meanwhile Macbeth opens the feast.
YOU KNOW YOUR OWN DEGREES - SIT DOWN: AT FIRST AND LAST, THE HEARTY WELCOME.
IS HE DISPATCH'D?
MOST ROYAL SIR, FLEANCE IS SCAPED.
MY LORD, HIS THROAT IS CUT.
THOU ART THE BEST O' TH' CUTTHROATS, YET HE'S GOOD THAT DID THE LIKE FOR FLEANCE.
MY ROYAL LORD, YOU DO NOT GIVE THE CHEER.
FROM THENCE, THE SAUCE TO MEAT IS CEREMONY, MEETING WERE BARE WITHOUT IT.

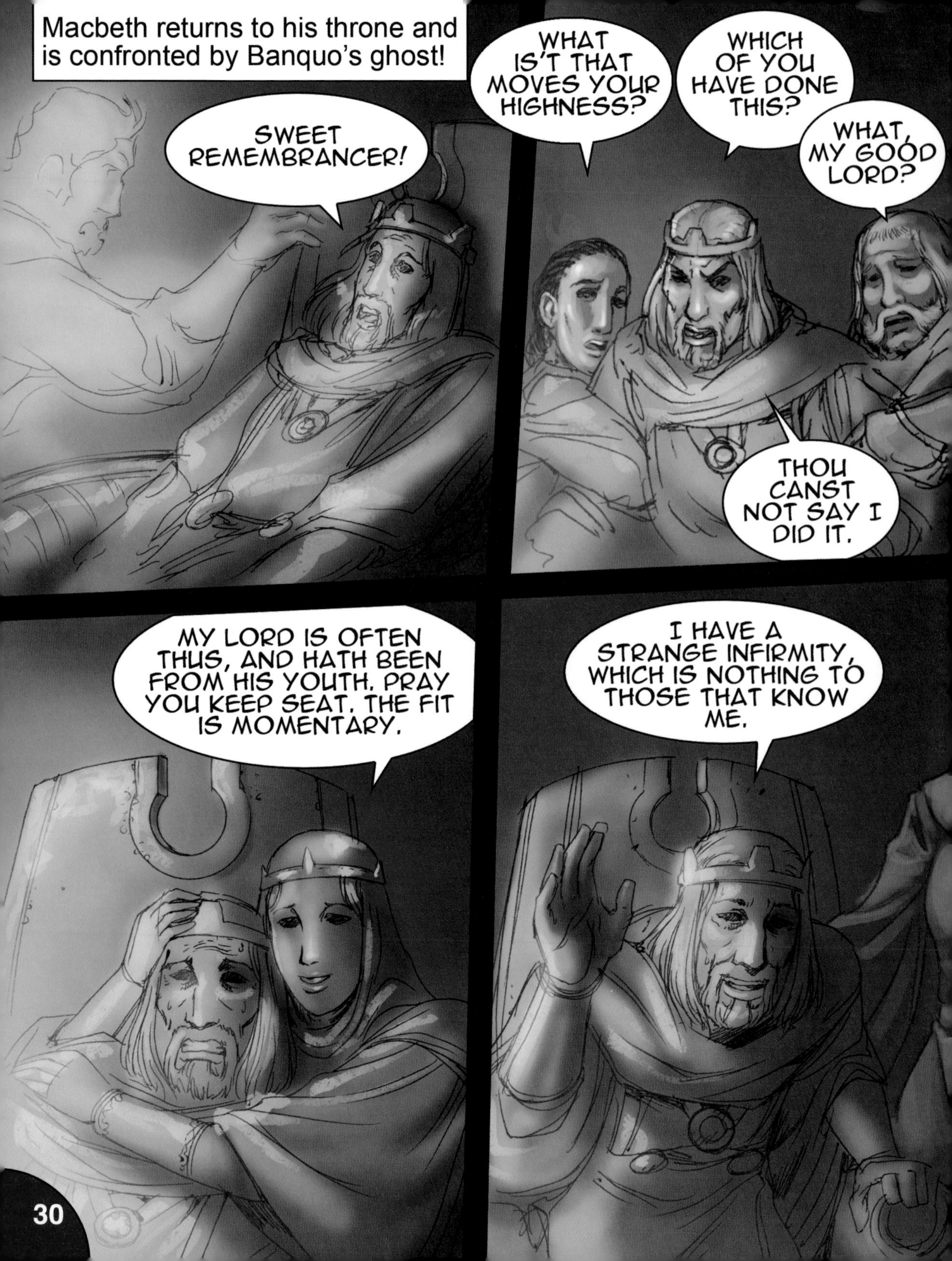
Macbeth returns to his throne and is confronted by Banquo's ghost!
SWEET REMEMBRANCER!
WHAT IS'T THAT MOVES YOUR HIGHNESS?
WHICH OF YOU HAVE DONE THIS?
WHAT, MY GOOD LORD?
THOU CANST NOT SAY I DID IT.
MY LORD IS OFTEN THUS, AND HATH BEEN FROM HIS YOUTH. PRAY YOU KEEP SEAT. THE FIT IS MOMENTARY.
I HAVE A STRANGE INFIRMITY, WHICH IS NOTHING TO THOSE THAT KNOW ME.

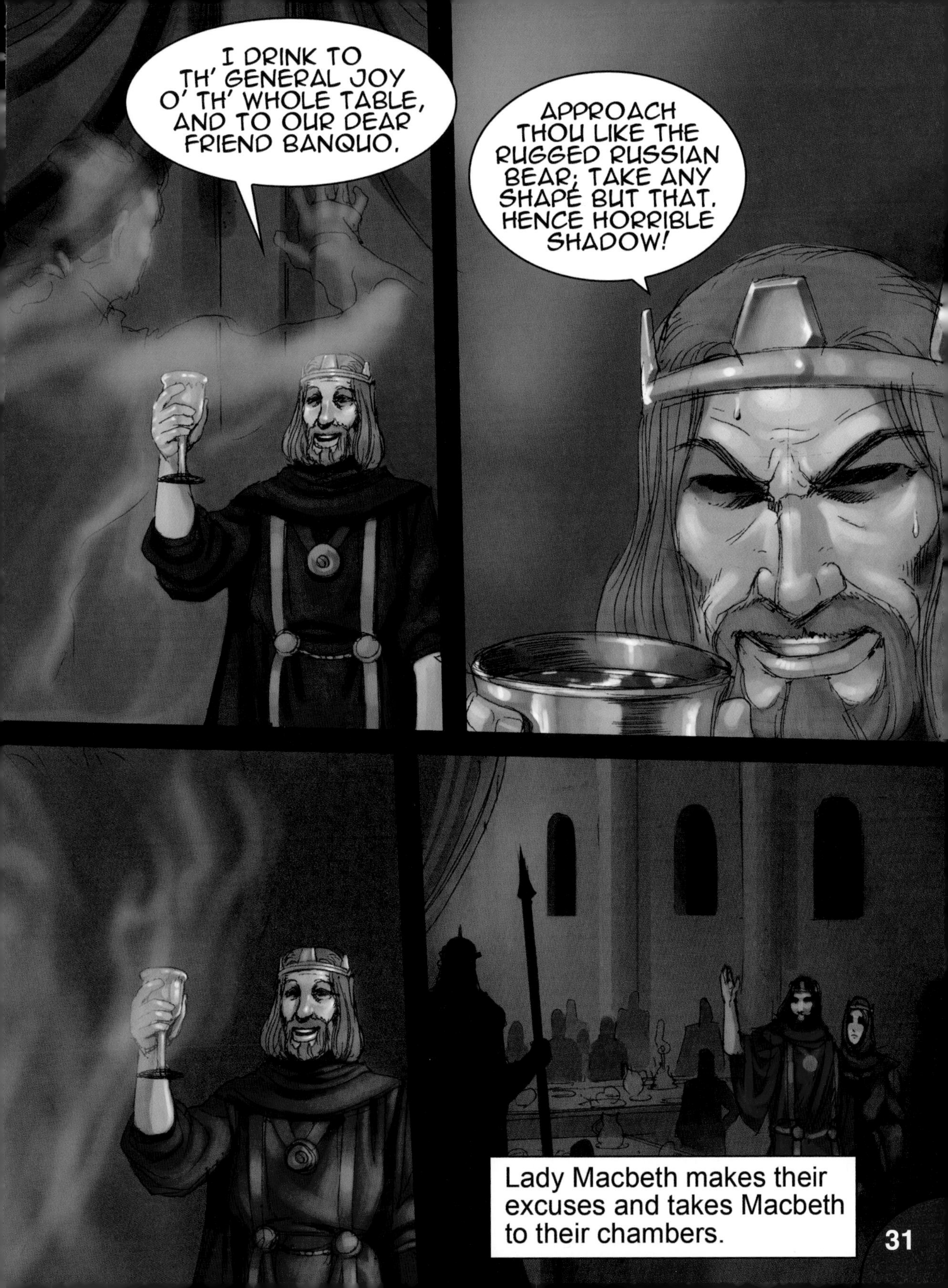
I DRINK TO TH' GENERAL JOY O' TH' WHOLE TABLE, AND TO OUR DEAR FRIEND BANQUO.
APPROACH THOU LIKE THE RUGGED RUSSIAN BEAR; TAKE ANY SHAPE BUT THAT. HENCE HORRIBLE SHADOW!
Lady Macbeth makes their excuses and takes Macbeth to their chambers.

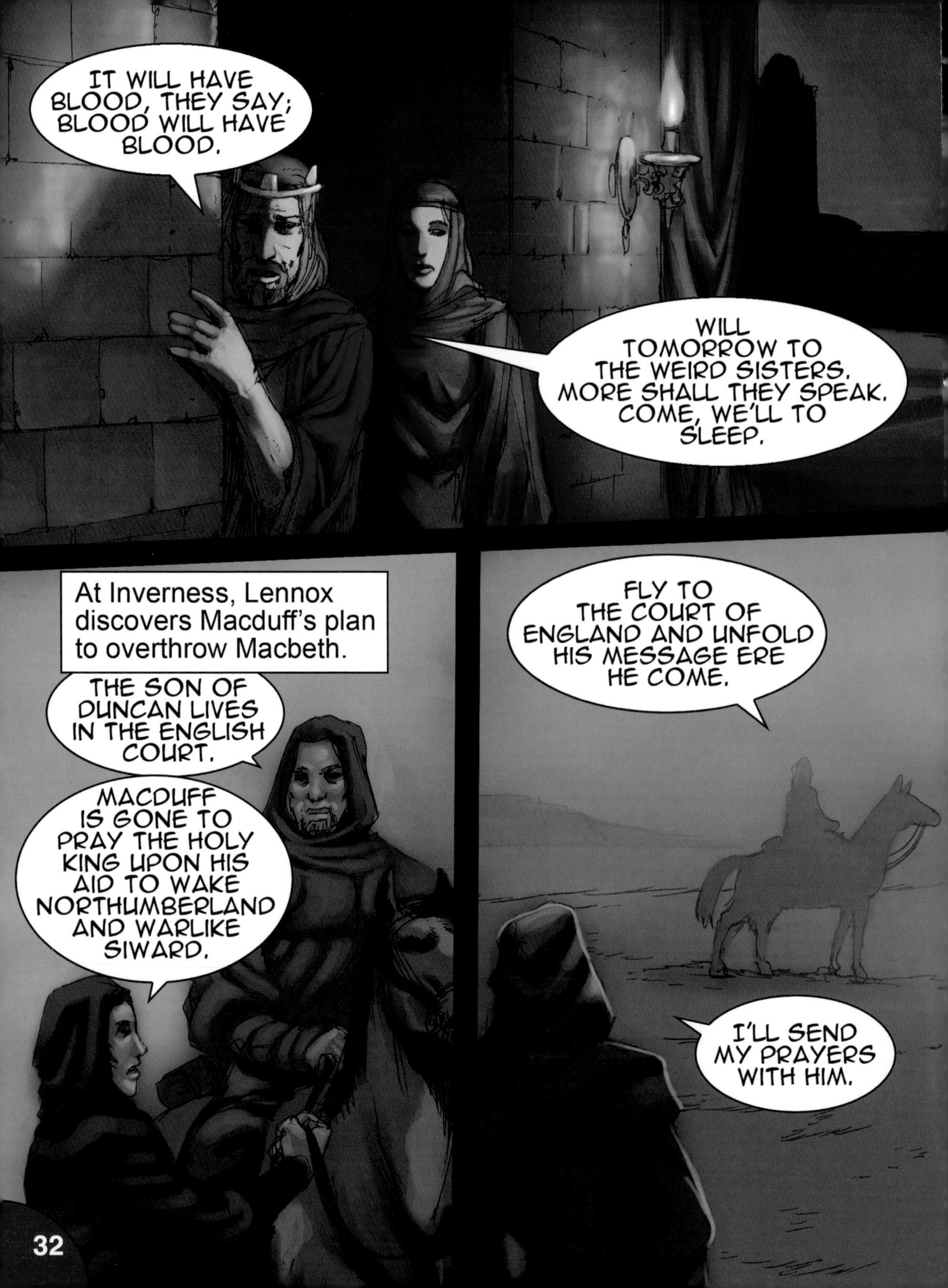
IT WILL HAVE BLOOD, THEY SAY; BLOOD WILL HAVE BLOOD.
WILL TOMORROW TO THE WEIRD SISTERS. MORE SHALL THEY SPEAK. COME, WE'LL TO SLEEP.
At Inverness, Lennox discovers Macduff's plan to overthrow Macbeth.
THE SON OF DUNCAN LIVES IN THE ENGLISH COURT.
MACDUFF IS GONE TO PRAY THE HOLY KING UPON HIS AID TO WAKE NORTHUMBERLAND AND WARLIKE SIWARD.
FLY TO THE COURT OF ENGLAND AND UNFOLD HIS MESSAGE ERE HE COME.
I'LL SEND MY PRAYERS WITH HIM.

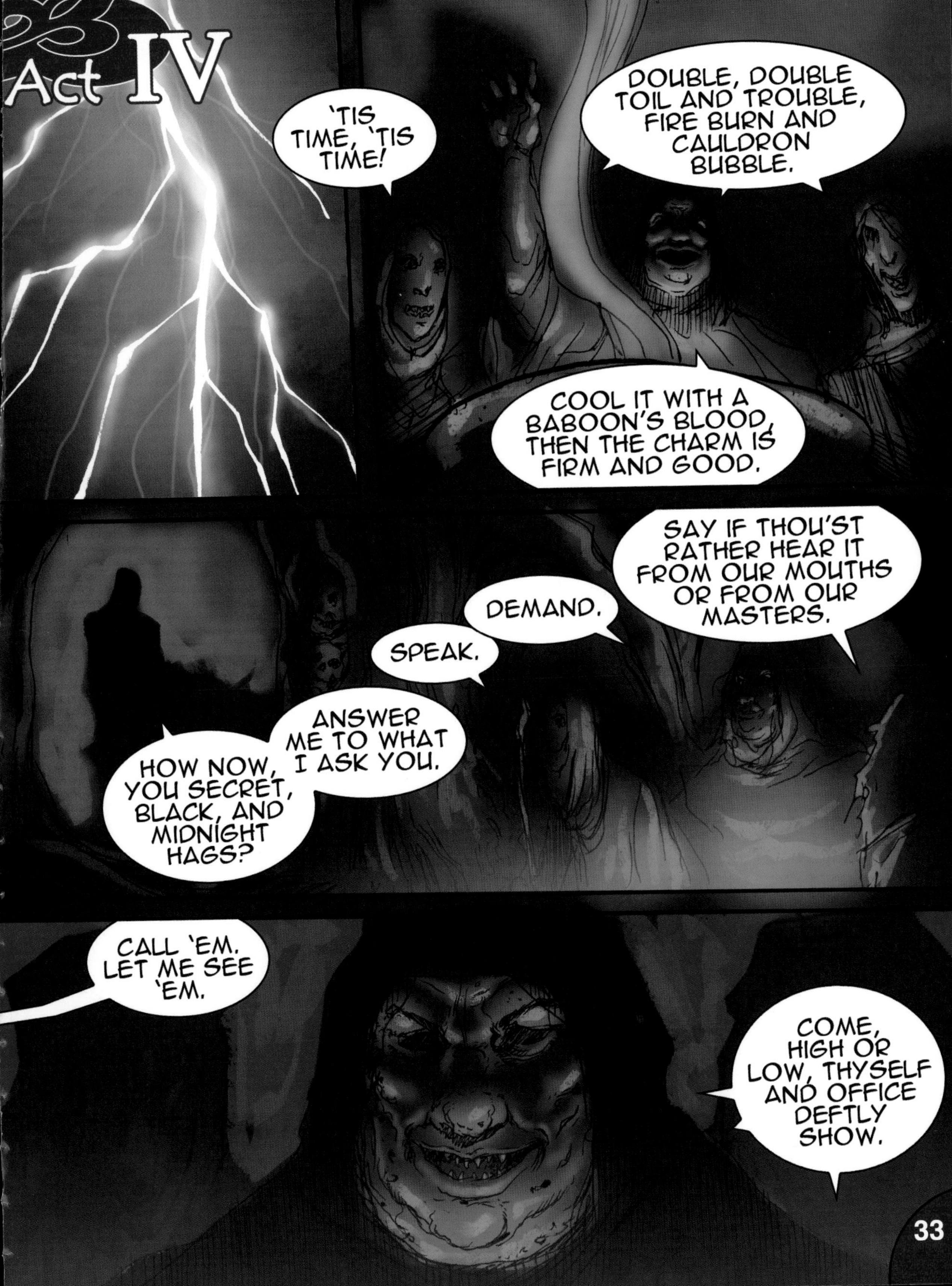
Act IV
'TIS TIME, 'TIS TIME!
DOUBLE, DOUBLE TOIL AND TROUBLE, FIRE BURN AND CAULDRON BUBBLE.
COOL IT WITH A BABOON'S BLOOD, THEN THE CHARM IS FIRM AND GOOD.
HOW NOW, YOU SECRET, BLACK, AND MIDNIGHT HAGS?
ANSWER ME TO WHAT I ASK YOU.
SPEAK.
DEMAND.
SAY IF THOU'ST RATHER HEAR IT FROM OUR MOUTHS OR FROM OUR MASTERS.
CALL 'EM. LET ME SEE 'EM.
COME, HIGH OR LOW, THYSELF AND OFFICE DEFTLY SHOW.

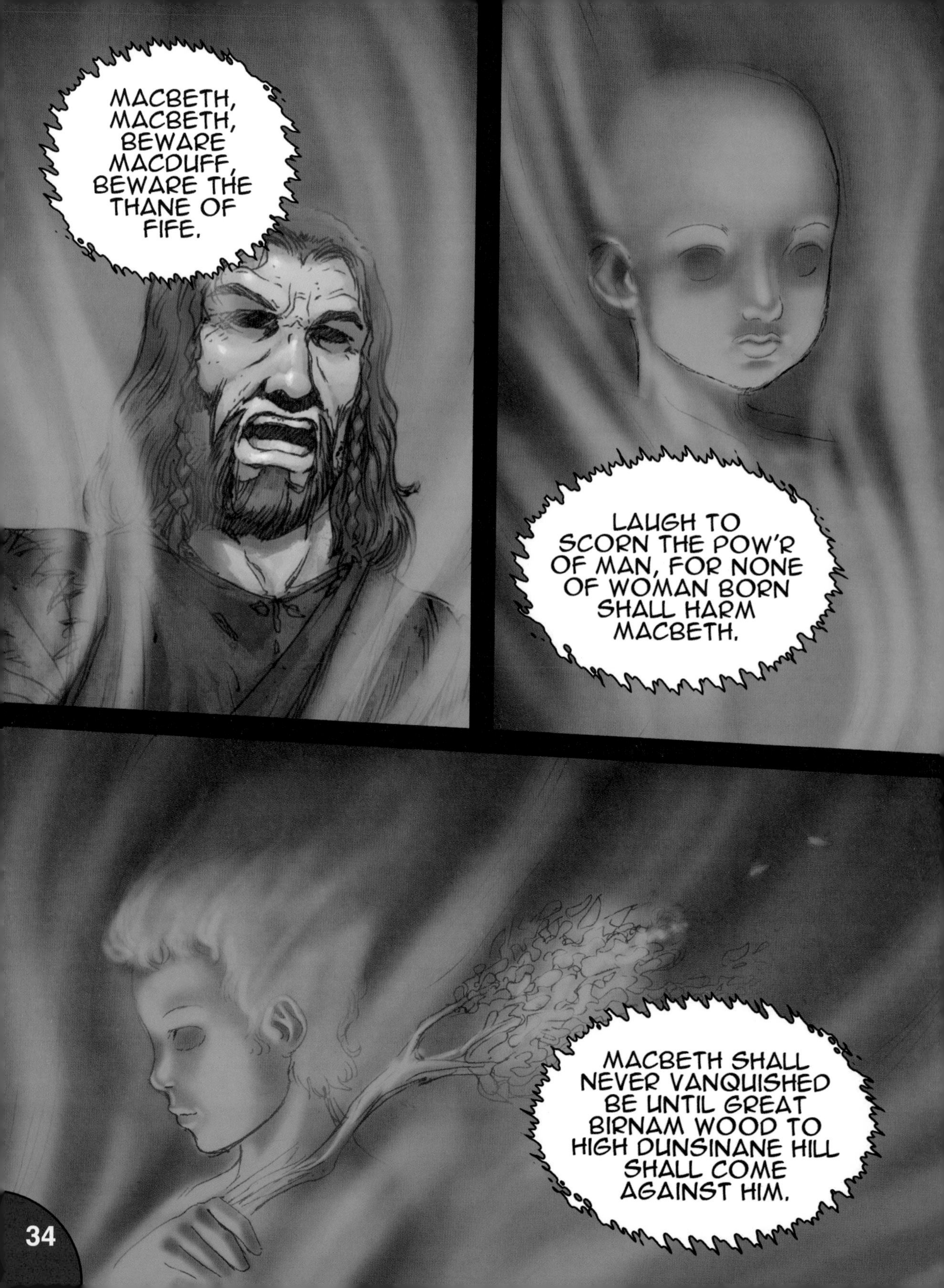
MACBETH, MACBETH, BEWARE MACDUFF, BEWARE THE THANE OF FIFE.
LAUGH TO SCORN THE POW'R OF MAN, FOR NONE OF WOMAN BORN SHALL HARM MACBETH.
MACBETH SHALL NEVER VANQUISHED BE UNTIL GREAT BIRNAM WOOD TO HIGH DUNSINANE HILL SHALL COME AGAINST HIM.

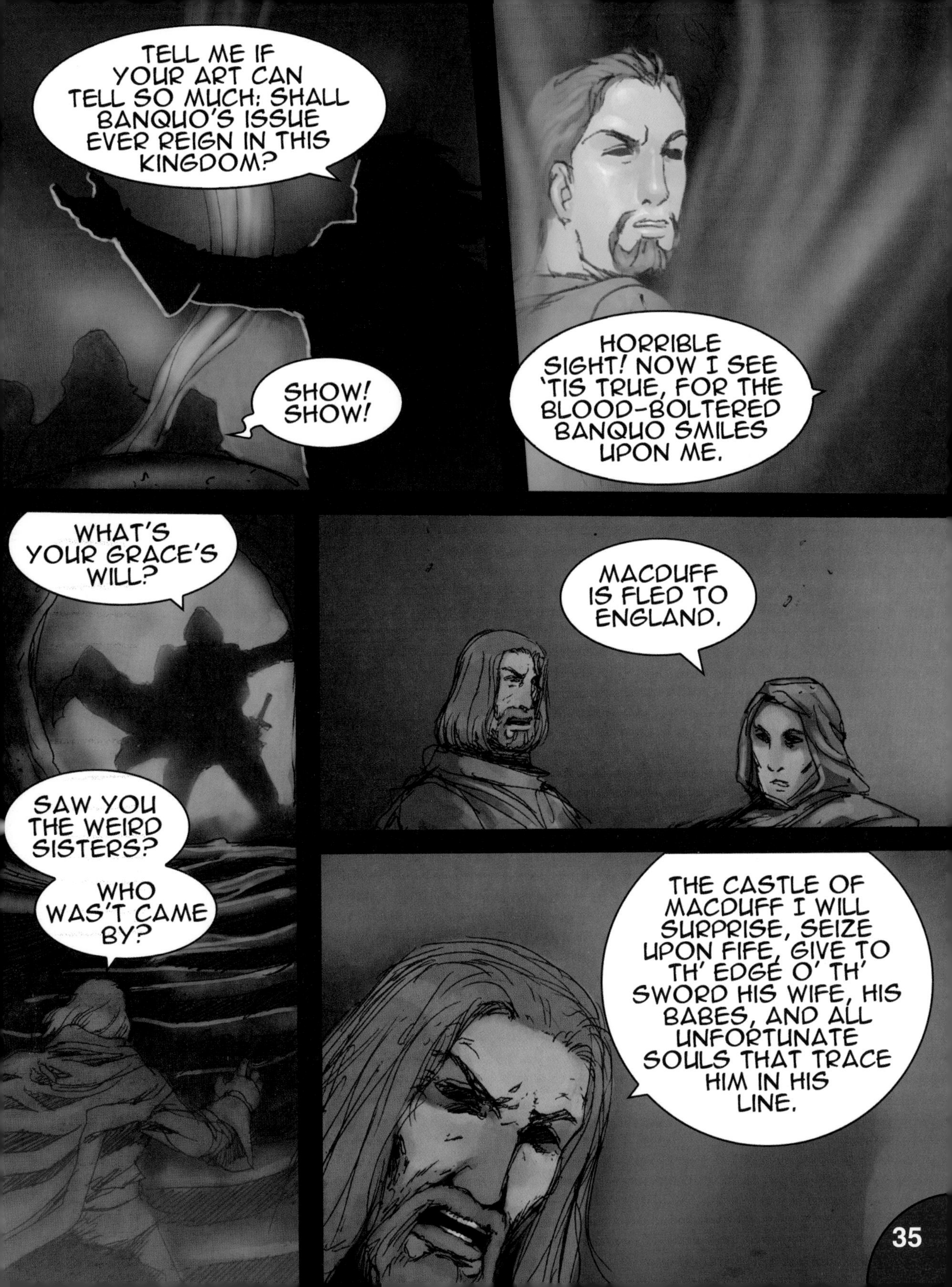
TELL ME IF YOUR ART CAN TELL SO MUCH: SHALL BANQUO'S ISSUE EVER REIGN IN THIS KINGDOM?
SHOW! SHOW!
HORRIBLE SIGHT! NOW I SEE 'TIS TRUE, FOR THE BLOOD-BOLTERED BANQUO SMILES UPON ME.
WHAT'S YOUR GRACE'S WILL?
SAW YOU THE WEIRD SISTERS?
WHO WAS'T CAME BY?
MACDUFF IS FLED TO ENGLAND.
THE CASTLE OF MACDUFF I WILL SURPRISE, SEIZE UPON FIFE, GIVE TO TH' EDGE O' TH' SWORD HIS WIFE, HIS BABES, AND ALL UNFORTUNATE SOULS THAT TRACE HIM IN HIS LINE.

Meanwhile, Malcolm and Macduff discuss Macbeth's climb to the throne.

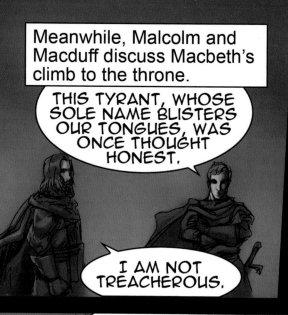

THIS TYRANT, WHOSE SOLE NAME BLISTERS OUR TONGUES, WAS ONCE THOUGHT HONEST.

I AM NOT TREACHEROUS.

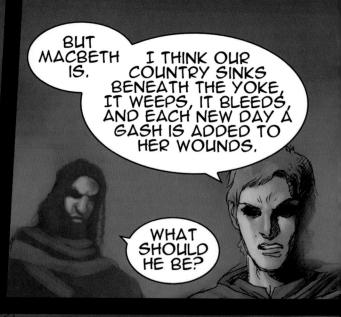

BUT MACBETH IS.

I THINK OUR COUNTRY SINKS BENEATH THE YOKE, IT WEEPS, IT BLEEDS, AND EACH NEW DAY A GASH IS ADDED TO HER WOUNDS.

WHAT SHOULD HE BE?

WERE I KING, I SHOULD CUT OFF THE NOBLES FOR THEIR LANDS, DESIRE HIS JEWELS, AND THIS OTHER'S HOUSE.

O SCOTLAND, SCOTLAND! THY ROYAL FATHER WAS A MOST SAINTED KING.

FARE THEE WELL. THESE EVILS REPEAT'ST UPON THYSELF.

WHAT I AM TRULY IS THINE AND MY POOR COUNTRY'S TO COMMAND.

MACDUFF, THIS NOBLE PASSION HATH RECONCILED MY THOUGHTS TO THY GOOD TRUTH AND HONOR.

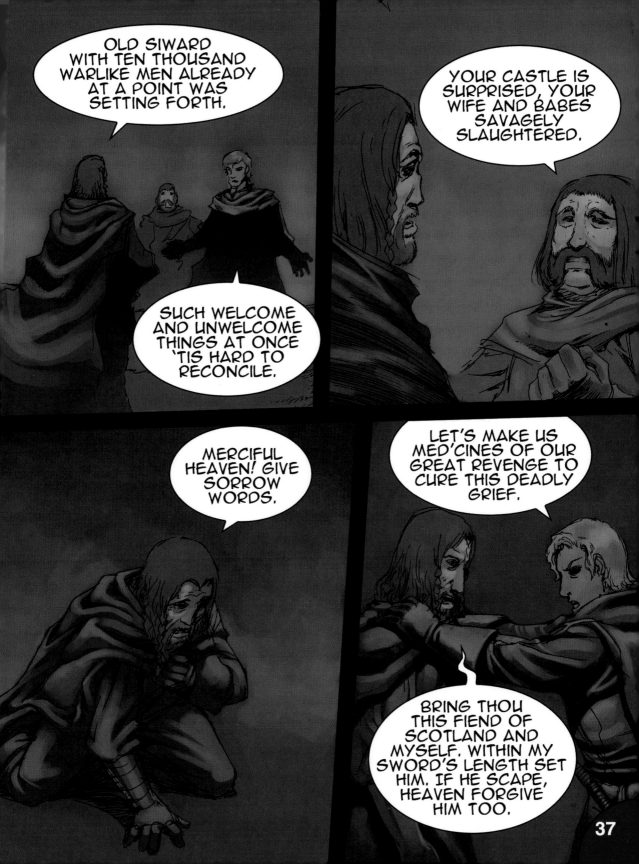

Act V

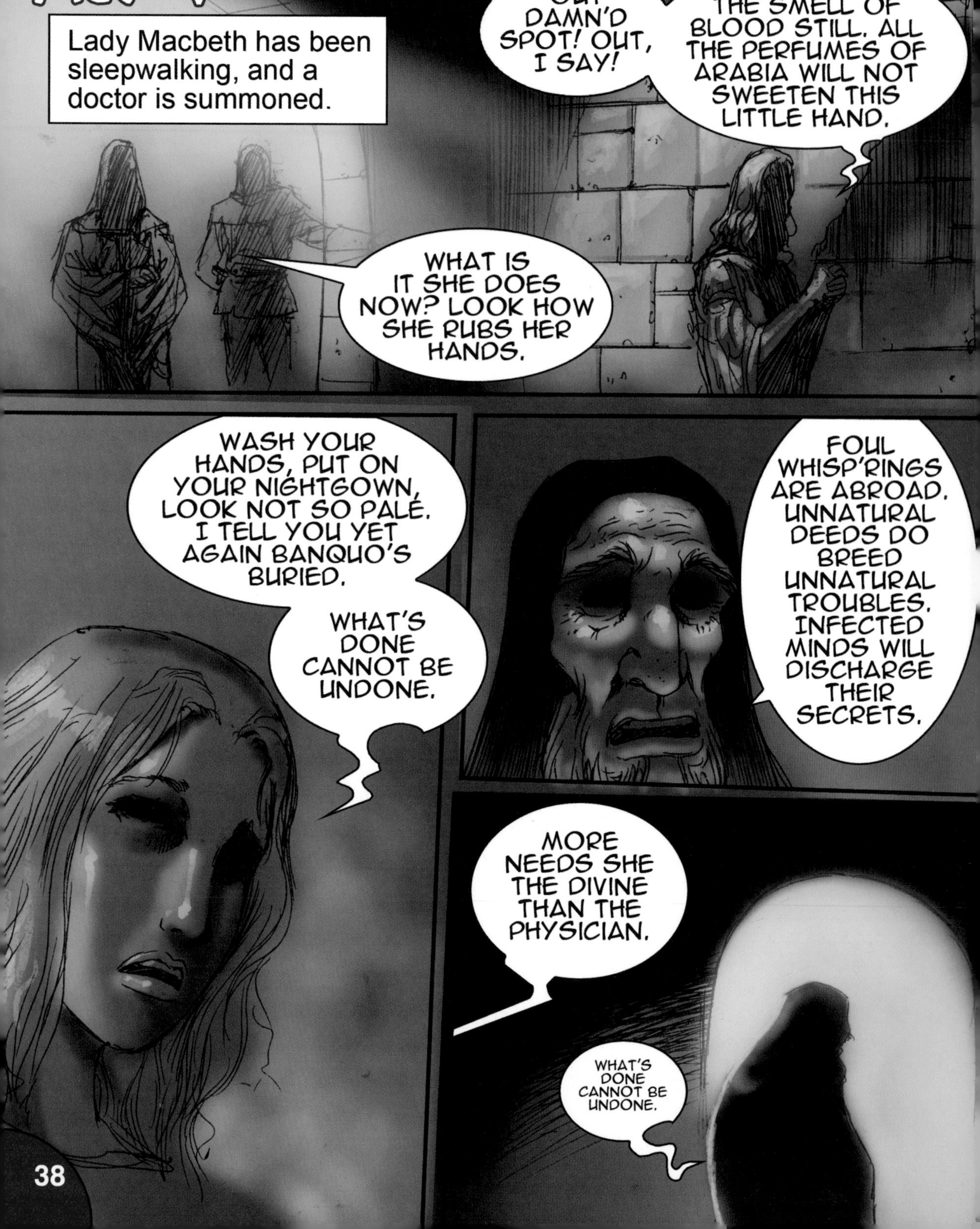

Lady Macbeth has been sleepwalking, and a doctor is summoned.
OUT DAMN'D SPOT! OUT, I SAY!
HERE'S THE SMELL OF BLOOD STILL. ALL THE PERFUMES OF ARABIA WILL NOT SWEETEN THIS LITTLE HAND.
WHAT IS IT SHE DOES NOW? LOOK HOW SHE RUBS HER HANDS.
WASH YOUR HANDS, PUT ON YOUR NIGHTGOWN, LOOK NOT SO PALE. I TELL YOU YET AGAIN BANQUO'S BURIED.
WHAT'S DONE CANNOT BE UNDONE.
FOUL WHISP'RINGS ARE ABROAD. UNNATURAL DEEDS DO BREED UNNATURAL TROUBLES. INFECTED MINDS WILL DISCHARGE THEIR SECRETS.
MORE NEEDS SHE THE DIVINE THAN THE PHYSICIAN.
WHAT'S DONE CANNOT BE UNDONE.

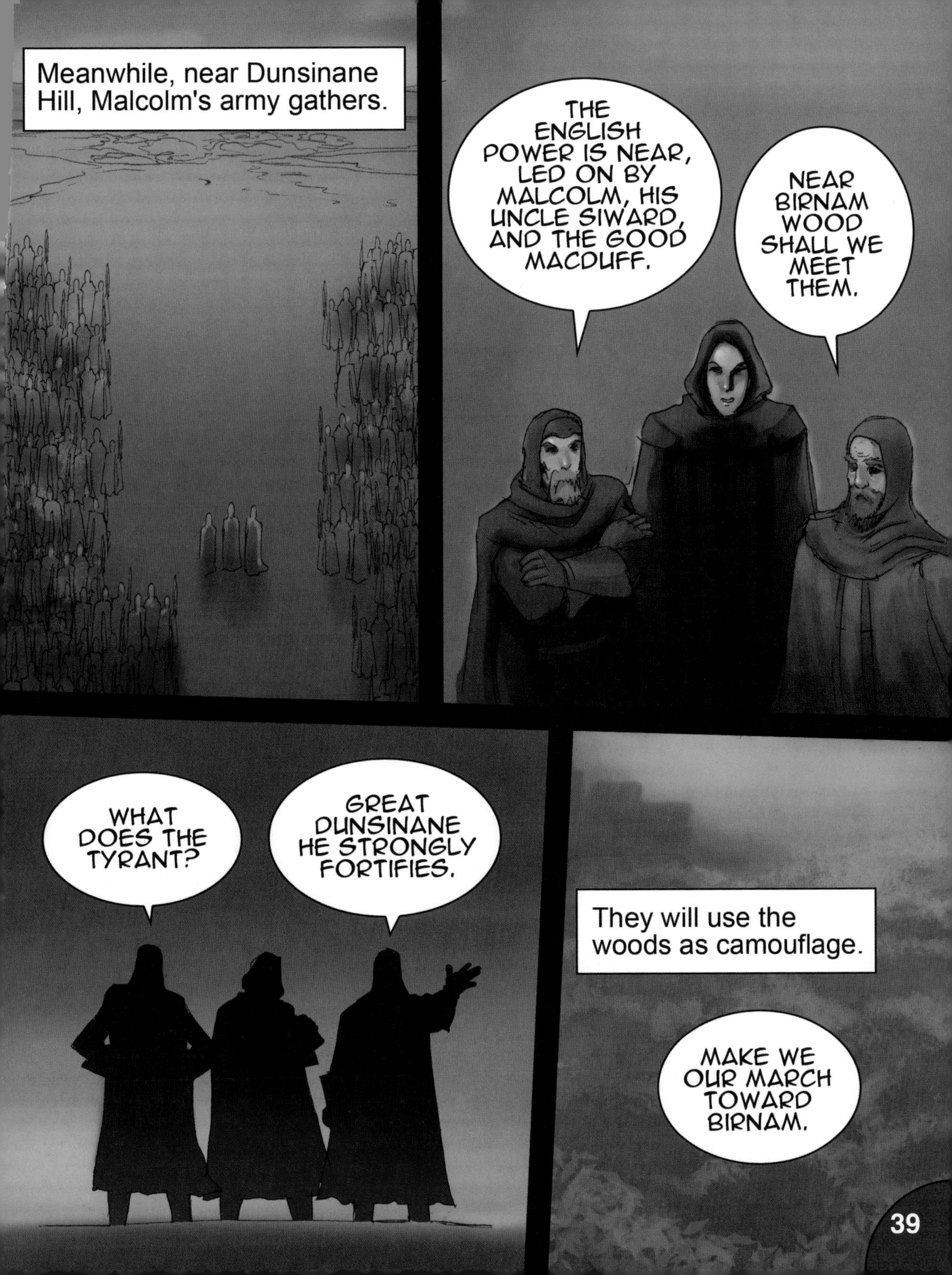
Meanwhile, near Dunsinane Hill, Malcolm's army gathers.
THE ENGLISH POWER IS NEAR, LED ON BY MALCOLM, HIS UNCLE SIWARD, AND THE GOOD MACDUFF.
NEAR BIRNAM WOOD SHALL WE MEET THEM.
WHAT DOES THE TYRANT?
GREAT DUNSINANE HE STRONGLY FORTIFIES.
They will use the woods as camouflage.
MAKE WE OUR MARCH TOWARD BIRNAM.

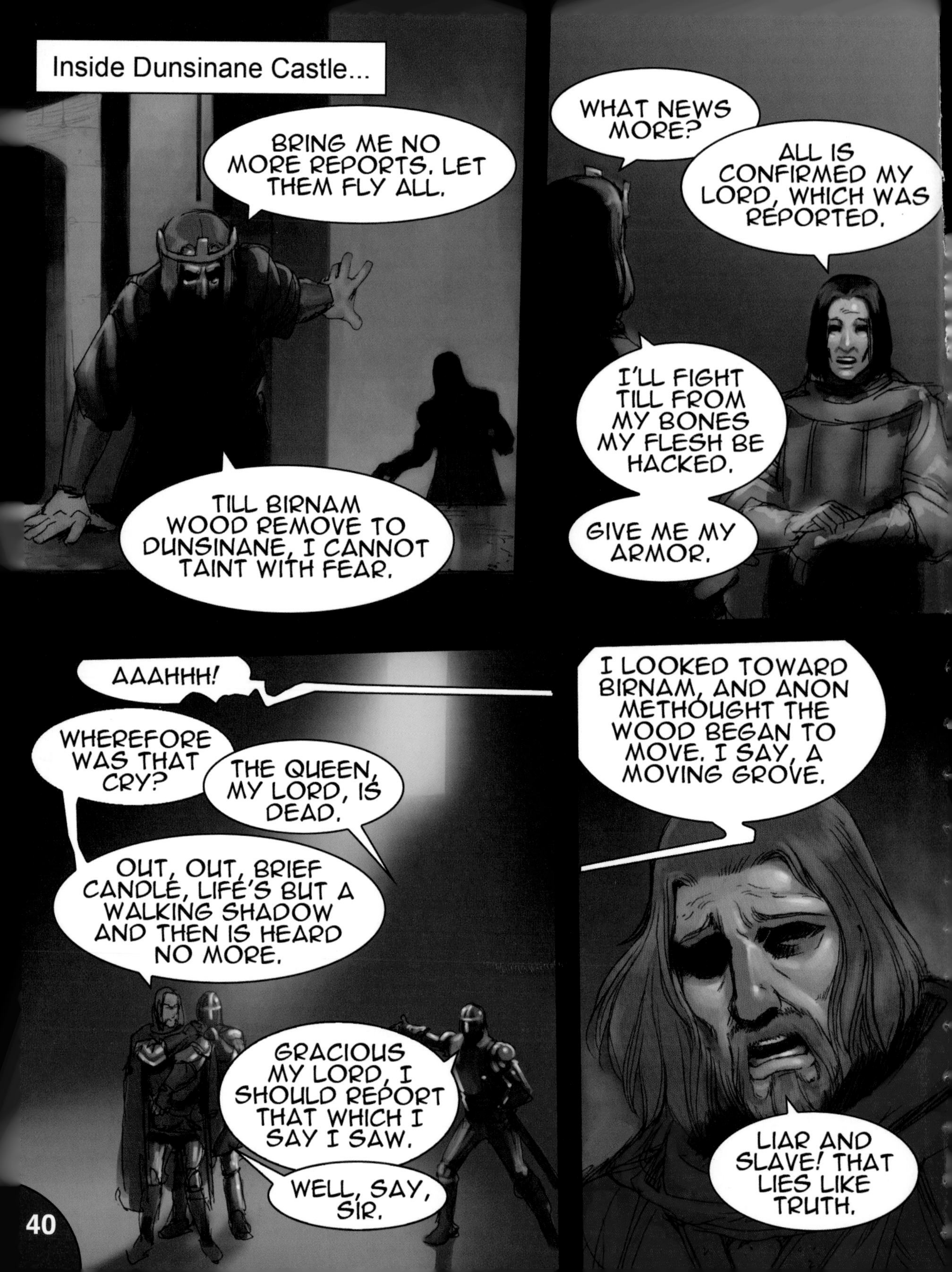
Inside Dunsinane Castle...
BRING ME NO MORE REPORTS. LET THEM FLY ALL.
TILL BIRNAM WOOD REMOVE TO DUNSINANE, I CANNOT TAINT WITH FEAR.
WHAT NEWS MORE?
ALL IS CONFIRMED MY LORD, WHICH WAS REPORTED.
I'LL FIGHT TILL FROM MY BONES MY FLESH BE HACKED.
GIVE ME MY ARMOR.
AAAHHH!
WHEREFORE WAS THAT CRY?
THE QUEEN, MY LORD, IS DEAD.
OUT, OUT, BRIEF CANDLE, LIFE'S BUT A WALKING SHADOW AND THEN IS HEARD NO MORE.
GRACIOUS MY LORD, I SHOULD REPORT THAT WHICH I SAY I SAW.
WELL, SAY, SIR.
I LOOKED TOWARD BIRNAM, AND ANON METHOUGHT THE WOOD BEGAN TO MOVE. I SAY, A MOVING GROVE.
LIAR AND SLAVE! THAT LIES LIKE TRUTH.

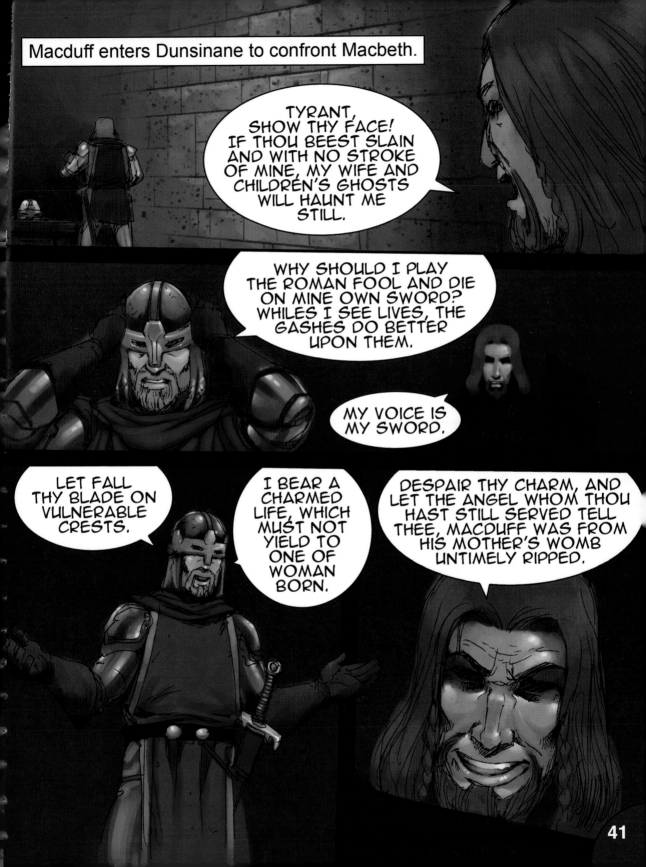

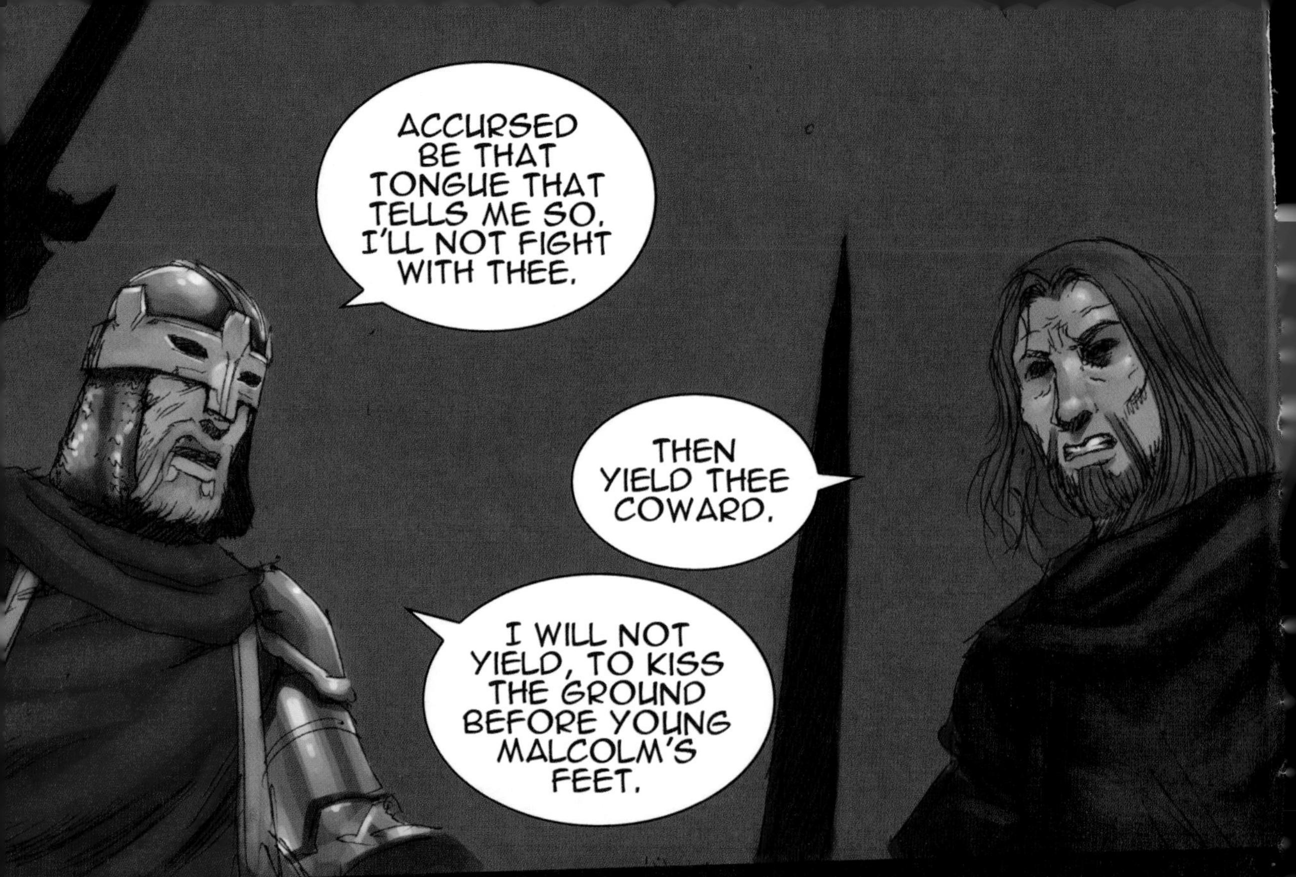
ACCURSED BE THAT TONGUE THAT TELLS ME SO. I'LL NOT FIGHT WITH THEE.
THEN YIELD THEE COWARD.
I WILL NOT YIELD, TO KISS THE GROUND BEFORE YOUNG MALCOLM'S FEET.

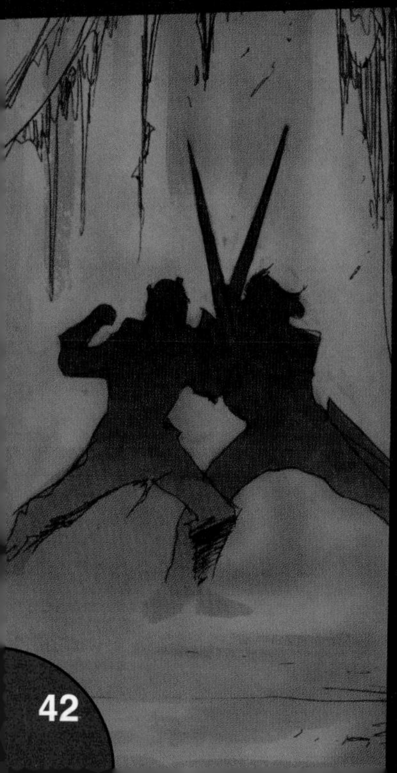

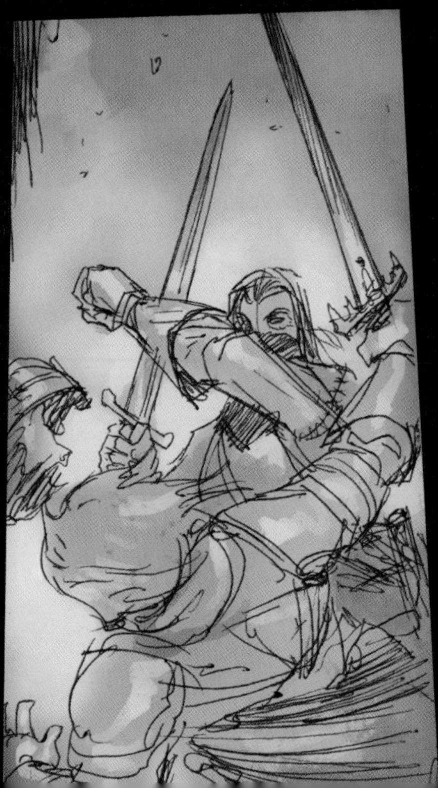

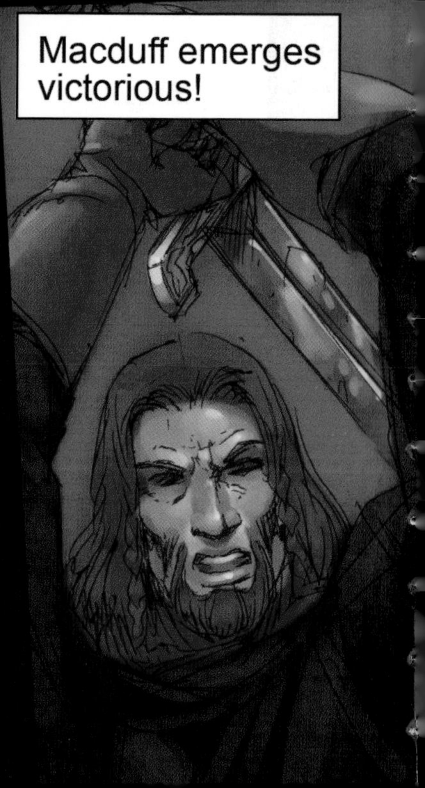
Macduff emerges victorious!

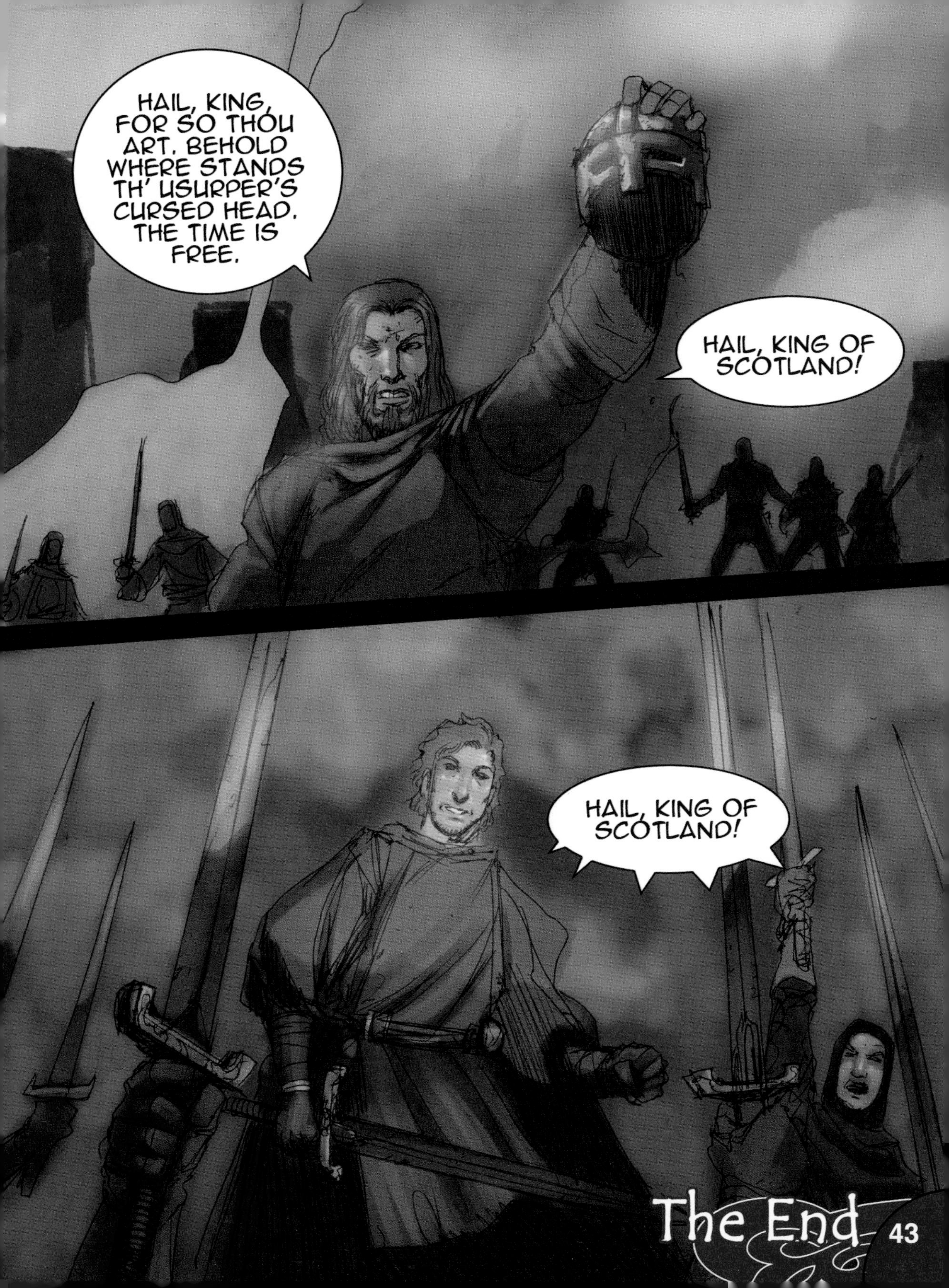
HAIL, KING, FOR SO THOU ART. BEHOLD WHERE STANDS TH' USURPER'S CURSED HEAD. THE TIME IS FREE.
HAIL, KING OF SCOTLAND!
HAIL, KING OF SCOTLAND!
The End

Behind Macbeth

Macbeth was written in about 1606 to 1607. It is part of Shakespeare's *First Folio*, which was printed in 1623. Some of text of the five-act tragedy was corrupt or not found for the *First Folio*. This may be why *Macbeth* is the shortest of Shakespeare's tragedies.

Shakespeare based *Macbeth* on the historical succession to the throne by Scottish general Macbeth. Macbeth was a Scottish noble who killed King Duncan I in battle at Eglin. Shakespeare adapted his story into a play of ambition and murder.

Macbeth opens with the three witches, or weird sisters, who foretell the future. Macbeth and Banquo meet the witches and are told that Macbeth will be thane of Cawdor and then king. Banquo is also told his sons will rule Scotland, though he will not.

Soon after, Duncan names Macbeth as thane of Cawdor. This leads Macbeth to believe the rest of the prophecy is true. When King Duncan visits Macbeth's castle, Macbeth and his wife decide it is time to kill the king and take over his throne.

Macbeth kills Duncan while he sleeps, and Lady Macbeth frames Duncan's servants. Macduff arrives early the next morning and discovers the murder. Soon after, Duncan's sons, Donalbain and Malcolm, flee, and Macbeth is named king.

Macbeth is threatened by Banquo's prophecy and arranges for Banquo and his son to be killed. Banquo's ghost haunts Macbeth while Lady Macbeth is driven mad by her part in the murder and soon dies. Meanwhile, Macduff joins Malcolm's army against Macbeth. Another part of the prophecy is fulfilled when Malcolm's army uses camouflage of Birnam Wood to advance on Macbeth's castle.

In the final battle, Macduff defeats Macbeth. The kingdom is then returned to the rightful king, Malcolm.

Since its beginning, *Macbeth* has been performed onstage throughout the world. There are also both film and television adaptations of this famous play.

Famous Phrases

By the pricking of my thumbs, something wicked this way comes.

But screw your courage to the sticking place and we'll not fail.

Double, double, toil and trouble, fire burn, and cauldron bubble.

Out damn'd spot! Out, I say!

Why do you dress me in borrowed robes?

About the Author

William Shakespeare was baptized on April 26, 1564, in Stratford-upon-Avon, England. At the time, records were not kept of births, however, the churches did record baptisms, weddings, and deaths. So, we know approximately when he was born. Traditionally, his birth is celebrated on April 23.

William was the son of John Shakespeare, a tradesman, and Mary Arden. He most likely attended grammar school and learned to read, write, and speak Latin.

Shakespeare did not go on to the university. Instead, he married Anne Hathaway at age 18. They had three children, Susanna, Hamnet, and Judith. Not much is known about Shakespeare's life at this time. By 1592 he had moved to London, and his name began to appear in the literary world.

In 1594, Shakespeare became an important member of Lord Chamberlain's company of players. This group had the best actors and the best theater, the Globe. For the next 20 years, Shakespeare devoted himself to writing. He died on April 23, 1616, but his works have lived on.

Additional Works by Shakespeare

The Comedy of Errors (1589–94)
The Taming of the Shrew (1590–94)
Romeo and Juliet (1594–96)
A Midsummer Night's Dream (1595–96)
Much Ado About Nothing (1598–99)
As You Like It (1598–1600)
Hamlet (1599–1601)
Twelfth Night (1600–02)
Othello (1603–04)
King Lear (1605–06)
Macbeth (1606–07)
The Tempest (1611)

About the Adapter

Joeming Dunn is both a general practice physician and the owner of one of the largest comic companies in Texas, Antarctic Press. A graduate of two Texas schools, Austin College in Sherman and the University of Texas Medical Branch in Galveston, he has currently settled in San Antonio.

David Hutchison is a creator, writer, and illustrator of graphic novels. Hutchison was born in Cincinnati, Ohio. His love of design and illustration began at an early age. Hutchison has worked in the fields of printing, mural painting, and portraiture. He resides in San Antonio, Texas, and has produced several graphic novels, including *Oz: The Manga*, *Mischief and Mayhem*, and *Dragon Arms*.

Glossary

accursed - being under a curse.

assault - a military attack involving direct contact.

furbished - renewed.

hurly-burly - the battle that is happening.

Neptune - the Roman god of the sea.

oracle - a priest or priestess through whom certain ancient gods, such as Apollo, answered the questions of their worshippers.

parley - to speak with another.

repentance - the act of feeling regret or sorrow for one's actions.

sacrilegious - dishonoring a sacred person, object, or place.

thane - a title for a Scottish noble.

wassail - bad behavior.

Web Sites

To learn more about William Shakespeare, visit ABDO Publishing Company on the World Wide Web at **www.abdopublishing.com**. Web sites about Shakespeare are featured on our Book Links page. These links are routinely monitored and updated to provide the most current information available.